Viviana Prado

7/23/16

# The Art of White Roses

*{ a novel }*

Viviana Prado-Núñez

Cover Design by Catherine Rosas-Huerta

Author Photograph by Viviana Prado-Núñez

Printed by CreateSpace in the United States of America

ISBN-13: 978-1530578078
ISBN-10: 1530578078

The author welcomes any comments or questions. For requests, feedback, or information, the author can be contacted at theartofwhiteroses@gmail.com.

*Para mi mamá y la abuela que nunca conocí*
For my mother and the grandmother I never knew

*Cultivo una rosa blanca*

Cultivo una rosa blanca,
en julio como en enero,
para el amigo sincero
que me da su mano franca.

Y para el cruel que me arranca
el corazón con que vivo,
cardo ni ortiga cultivo;
cultivo la rosa blanca.

— José Martí

*I Grow a White Rose*

I grow a white rose,
in July as in January,
for the sincere friend who
gives me his honest hand.

And for the cruel one who tears
from me the heart with which I live,
thorn nor thistle do I grow;
I grow the white rose.

— José Martí

# { Contents }

The air must have been quiet, light and fresh the way it never was in the daytime. No gunshots that night. The clouds blocking the sky like a screen door. In the Hotel, a few curtains were open and laughter dribbled out as people held drinks in the windows. They were oblivious. The men in the casino wore tuxedos and the women wore glittery gold dresses that gleamed in the rawness of the light. The others watched television in their hotel rooms, and their children took baths in rooms made of tile. Outside, the red roofs were dim in the dark and the trees were twisted as if loving each other. There were cement walkways between them and, though it didn't seem that way, the grass was green and alive.

On one of the walkways was Miguel. It was the end of his shift, and out he came by the staff entrance as the luminescence of the pool shone up to the palm trees. I'd seen pools before in the rich parts of town like Miramar, but this one I pictured special – a hole in the ground five cars wide filled with deep turquoise water. I imagined Miguel with his backpack slung over his shoulder, his good black shoes tied and dangling around his neck. His feet squelched in the mud and he was having trouble walking.

Then, from behind the brick wall a harsh glow. Headlights. Tires screeching. A small black shadow against the gloom, lobbed quickly. It landed in the squelch and – BOOM!

His ears, they must've hurt so much. The air probably sucked from his lungs, his head pining for oxygen, his vision shaking. I could imagine the slowness of it. Him raising his head, the mud warm and gooey on his cheek. And, suddenly, all of it going backwards. Rolling, my cousin Miguel rolling, the mud on his elbows like playing baseball in the rain. But slow, so slow, you could see the bits of Hotel grass getting mushed beneath his fingernails.

When he got up, his whole body buzzing with the pounding, the shrapnel must have been scattered all around: a piece in his backpack, the trunk and leaves of a palm tree so decimated he felt like crying. And he did cry, I'm sure of it, though he would always deny it. Right then and there, he cried like a kid and I knew because I saw the tracks on his cheeks when he came back, tracing through the mud.

Tía Carmen was in hysterics.

She'd been that way all evening, and even though she lived a few houses down, she still sat on the couch in our living room, praying under her breath the way nuns at Catholic school did if we used God's name in vain. On most days, Miguel came home by six, and even though he'd said he was going to have a late shift, she'd started panicking at eight. And so, she'd come over from her house with her mascara running and her Bible, making the sign of the cross so many times I thought her arms would fall off.

Tía Carmen was small, with mousy brown hair and creases on her forehead like wrinkled paper. As she sat on our couch and cried, her wrinkles etched themselves deep into her forehead. In the kitchen, Mami was anxious. She stood barefoot by the stove, which was mint-green and smelled of gas. Her hair was dark and she had on a nightgown that needed ironing. She didn't even turn on the radio as she sat cooking, watching a slice of ham sizzle in the saucepan.

Tía Carmen sobbed. "He's dead, disappeared! Gone like Rafi Consuelo. In the dead of night they took him. No note, no explanations – just vanished."

"Carmen, stop it," Mami said. "Don't say things like that. It's bad luck."

"But you know it's true, you know it. When someone goes missing, never seen again. All of them gone. It's already nine o'clock and Miguel's not back yet. *Mi pobre Miguel, mi ángel.*" From his big green armchair, Abuelo rolled his eyes. "*Lo juro por Dios*, every time a pin drops, that woman cries."

"*Ay, cállate*, Papá," Mami said.

I stood silent at the doorway, watching. I wasn't sure whether to be scared or not. Abuelo must have seen an odd expression on my face because he patted the arm of his armchair.

"Come here, Delita."

I sat where he told me like I usually did, leaning into him. I was getting too big for this.

"Don't be scared, Dela," Abuelo told me, "Your Tía is just having another nervous breakdown."

Mami pressed down on the ham with a spatula. She lifted it and folded it onto a piece of bread. She stared at the plate and seemed sick. She pushed it away.

"Mami, where's Papi?" I asked.

"What?"

"Papi. He should be home by now, shouldn't he?"

"Yes, well... I'm sure he had some things to tie up at the shop. Adela, it's getting late. Why don't you go to your room and check on Pingüino?"

Abuelo watched the black-and-white TV. It was a western, but the volume was so low we could still hear Tía Carmen's whimpers. She was rocking back and forth, murmuring prayers louder than before. I wished he would turn it up.

"Good night, Abuelo." I gave him a kiss on the cheek before leaving.

In my room, time trickled by too slowly. The skinny hand on the clock quivered each time it ticked. Hours passed. I switched on the lamp. There was no Papi or Miguel. Pingüino was sprawled out on his back on the bed across from me, asking stupid questions like "Do you think he's dead?" and "Do you think if he's dead, Tío Rodrigo would let me have his baseball bat?"

"Shut up," I told him. "What if he's really dead?"

For a moment, Pingüino was serious. Then he chuckled. "Please. Knowing Miguel, he probably got held back drooling after some *chica* way out of his league."

"You're disgusting, you know that?"

"So are you."

"So did you do it?"

"What?"

"The lizards."

"Yes."

"What happened?"

Pingüino laughed. "Lots of screaming. The usual."

"What happens when Mami finds out?"

"She won't."

I sat up in bed and leaned against the wall. It was humid tonight and the ceiling fan wasn't on yet, so my skin stuck to my shirt and the wall was moist. I squinted at Pingüino's school uniform he hadn't changed out of because he was too lazy. I sighed.

"Where's the letter?"

Pingüino observed the ceiling. "What letter?"

"I'm not stupid, Pingüino. This is the third time, and there's always a letter home the third time around. Where is it?"

"I ripped it."

"What?"

"And threw it in a bush. At Rafi Consuelo's house."

"Are you insane? You know not to go there. What if someone had seen you?"

"They didn't. Calm down for God's sake."

I put my face in my hands and watched him through my fingers. "You are dead. When Mami finds out…"

"She won't. Besides, everyone's worrying about Miguel, so no one would've cared anyway. Relax, Adela."

"You can't use Miguel as an excuse. You don't know what's happened to him. He could be dead or lying shot in an alleyway or something. And Lord knows where Papi is. For all we know they could both be —"

"Can we stop talking about them that way? Miguel is fine. He's got to be. And Papi... he probably got held up at work or something."

Fear pulsated in the air. If someone had stalked across the lawn and cracked the window open, they would have heard our hearts beating dull and muted, like the echo of someone tapping their fingers on the other side of a wall.

Eleven o'clock. The front door creaked open. There was a strangled cry from Tía Carmen.

When Pingüino and I got to the living room, Miguel was at the door, hollow with fear. His eyes were broken mirrors. Tío Rodrigo came in and his face sagged from tiredness. He sniffed the air.

"Do you have any food? I'm starving."

The scene could have belonged in a painting. In our living room with its flower print curtains my grandmother made, Tío Rodrigo stood large and hunkering in his blue police uniform, a steady mellow presence like a wall made of concrete. Abuelo sat shriveled as a prune in his green chair, his glasses glinting in the lamplight. Mami had dragged in the stool from the kitchen and sat with her hands covering her mouth. Pingüino lingered by my side, his hair flat at the back from having lain in the bed staring at the ceiling. He gazed at Miguel as if he were a stranger. On the couch, Tía Carmen smoothed out Miguel's hair and the wrinkles in his clothes and fussed at the grass stains. She was, not surprisingly, in tears. "I'm fine, Mami," Miguel said, scooting away, but his hands shook. "I'm fine." He saw me and Pingüino and smiled, relieved almost.

"Hey Pingüino. Hey Adela... The weather's shit, isn't it?"

"Hey Miguel," Pingüino said, and there was a flicker of a smile. I laughed, but went straight-faced in case that wasn't the right thing to do.

Just last week, the Presidential Palace had been attacked and Tío Rodrigo was one of the police officers on duty. President Batista was on the third floor with a gun in one hand and a telephone in the other and people in the streets were getting shot at while a man on the radio screamed that Batista was dead even though he wasn't. Papi was working in the shoe shop when it happened, and he said it was a miracle the windows didn't shatter. He got a bunch of strangers cowering behind the counters and he said it was a miracle too none of them had tried to rob him. One woman who'd run in said she'd almost been shot in the head, that the bullet had rebounded off the wall behind her and she'd seen a whole group of people gunned down by police at the corner of Colon and Prado. Afterwards, the tanks had been called in, and even now they crawled over the city like giant green bugs. I didn't see anything when it happened because I was in school. We'd been pulled out and everything, although I'm not sure why. We didn't live anywhere near the Presidential Palace.

Instead we lived in Marianao, a suburb six miles away from Old Havana. Most people in our neighborhood were poor and they couldn't read. There was a beach a few minutes away, but the sand was grainy and the sea rough despite being the right shade of green. In the Plaza, there was a big marble statue in the center and if it weren't for the people and the butcher shop, it could pass for being respectable. But the whole place stunk of blood and meat, and beggars stooped at the curbs. Thankfully, our street wasn't like that so we never strayed far. I loved our house especially. It was small – one story high with a concrete porch and blue walls on the outside. In the back, we had a yard cramped with mango trees because Papi's father used to own a sugarcane plantation and Papi's favorite thing about it had been the small batch of mango trees near the front door. His parents were all dead and now, it was Tía Noelia, her husband, and her four kids who ran the place in Oriente. We'd never been because it was on the other side of the island near the Sierra Maestra, the mountains where all the rebels were supposed to be.

Miguel would've come home later but for the fact that Tío Rodrigo was a policeman and knew how to deal with those kinds of things. When Tía Carmen asked who had done it, Tío Rodrigo claimed it was a couple of rebel kids messing around as usual. And even though it wasn't much of an explanation, it was enough. Ever since I could remember, the newspapers had had pictures in them of dead bodies riddled with bullets. It was the rebels, Papi told me. It was Fidel Castro's men dying. I didn't pretend to understand much about the rebellion, but I knew none of it was very good. Fidel was the rebel in Oriente who shot people and Batista was the president in Havana who tortured them. Every so often, there were stories of Batista's blue-helmeted police who plucked people off the streets and tortured them for days on end, or shot down an entire family and left a survivor to keep the fear going. They liked to march through the city in rows, guns aloft, blue uniforms crisp like their mothers had ironed them that morning. It was hard figuring out who was right or wrong in this thing. Batista was bad because Papi said so and Castro... No one talked about whether Castro was good or not.

Of course, those boys in Oriente would fail. It was inevitable. Batista had been in power much too long for things to change. No matter how many pictures in the newspaper showed Batista walking through crowds of Cubans weeping at his feet, kissing babies in their mothers' arms, riding in the passenger's side of an open-roofed car with his shining canine smile, everyone knew hell would freeze over before Batista gave up being president, before anything in Cuba changed. But no one said these things in the open. People wore fear on their faces, when they walked on the street, when they went to get groceries. They jumped when an engine backfired. No one would ever talk because it might mean being the next corpse in the newspaper.

"Everything is okay. Whoever did this, we'll catch them," Tío Rodrigo said in his quiet way. He gazed at Miguel and Tía Carmen on the couch. "I promise."

After Tío Rodrigo had eaten his fill and Tía Carmen had calmed herself down, they went home. From the window, I watched them walk towards the corner leading to their house. I stayed there a while, gazing at the empty street, the way the streetlights made everything mysterious, the way the humidity drifted in through the window. Straining my eyes, waiting for the glint of the hood on Papi's car, watching Tío Rodrigo's hunched back round the corner. And I wondered, I couldn't help wondering, about how many things Tío Rodrigo had lied about.

## 2 The Other Adela

That night, I woke up at one in the morning in a cold sweat. I had
had a dream about a bearded rebel who shot Papi and Miguel at
the Hotel Nacional. In the background, Tío Rodrigo watched from
a police car parked underneath a palm tree, Batista smiling his
canine smile in the backseat.

It was a gunshot night. I could hear them pop-pop-popping in
the distance, long moments of silence in between, and then a
sudden spurt of violence punctuating the air. I observed Pingüino's
sleeping form, envious, as I listened to his steady breathing. I
concentrated on the whoosh of the ceiling fan, on Pingüino's
school uniform he had abandoned in the middle of the floor, on
our closet that held only a few changes of clothes for the both of us.
I stared at the ceiling and how the moon elongated the shadows of
things. I jiggled my foot under the covers, waiting to fall asleep. I
couldn't.

When I trudged into the living room, the light from the black-
and-white TV was washing over everything, making it all gray and
ghostly. Abuelo sat on the couch, his green armchair deserted in
the corner. There was no one else, but he sat right up against the
arm nearest to the television and left the rest of the couch empty as
if he were waiting for more people to join him. He was very small.

He raised his head.

"I had a bad dream."

Abuelo didn't speak. Instead, he patted the place next to him,
and I curled up against his side. His clothes smelled of tobacco and
coconut water the way they always did. There was another western

on and I watched it with my eyelids drooping, pretending the gunshots in the distance were coming from the television. On the mantel were the family pictures: Mami when she was a little girl on a tricycle with streamers. Mami and Papi's wedding day, and them on the front stairs of our house in Marianao. Me as a toddler peering over at baby Pingüino in his crib. Papi's big plantation family lined up for a portrait in front of the sugarcane fields. The *abuela* I was named after, smiling next to the mango trees.

I began thinking of her – my grandmother.

I was born July 30, 1943, three days after my grandmother, also Adela, died of cancer. When I came, Abuelo called me a miracle because I had her green eyes and dark blond hair, so he said they should name me after her. And they did. But my eyes weren't a pretty green like characters in books. They were muddy like pond water – a green you mistook for brown until you looked more closely. My hair was okay. It wasn't a bright blond like the *americanas* in films, but it wasn't my Mami's hair either, black and rippling. It was an in-between like my eyes, something no one could put their finger on. I wondered if Abuela Adela felt that way about herself, but I suppose I would never know. It was far too late for that.

There were other things I wondered about her too. Like if she felt this lost at my age. I didn't believe in ghosts, but when I was smaller, I used to imagine she was hovering nearby, listening to my thoughts, wanting to give me advice, but staying inevitably silent. Then I stopped imagining because I thought that was dishonest and that people should only imagine ghosts if they believed in them.

There was no one else who was thirteen and lonely. The other kids in my class didn't like thinking. They liked cursing when the nuns weren't listening and calling each other *pingas*. They liked ignoring the rebellion and buying sugar-crumbled churros from the black man with the cart who sold them after school. I just did my schoolwork and then came home and listened to Miguel and

Pingüino annoying each other while people claimed the world was falling apart. I didn't feel like the world was falling apart though. I felt more like I was floating helpless in space, trying to keep track of where was up and where was down and feeling very wrong sometimes. And all the while I tried not to imagine the dead grandmother I was named after floating nearby and smiling bittersweetly.

"Abuelo, do you miss her?"

He tore his eyes from the television and gazed at the picture of her on the mantel. In it, she was still beautiful: lips plump, pretty teeth in a crescent moon, eyes piercing through the black-and-white. She hadn't become skin-and-bones yet. She was happy.

"All the time, Delita." He stroked my hair. "All the time."

That was the great thing about Abuelo. He didn't ask questions, only answered them. He let you put your head in his lap, stroked your hair until you fell asleep, and didn't say a word.

The disappearance of Rafi Consuelo was a neighborhood mystery. It had happened around three weeks ago, like Tía Carmen had said, in the dead of night. The only witness was Señor Moreno, the old man who lived on the corner, smack-dab in the middle of the intersection. It was three o'clock in the morning and he was outside on his porch, smoking a cigar after having been woken by the barking of a faraway dog.

Señor Moreno lived alone, in the house nearest to Havana on the east side, and on that night, the sky was windless and sweeping. He saw a sleek black car drive down the street and park itself on the curb in front of Rafi Consuelo's house. He remembered noticing because it was a nice car and nice cars weren't something you saw outside of the city, unless it was going to the cabaret or the racetrack nearby.

But there it was. It had stopped right there and soon enough, he heard a resounding knock. Then Rafi Consuelo answered this strange man in the night.

Rafi Consuelo was a new addition to the street. He was young, somewhere in his twenties, and had moved into the house last November after the University of Havana closed due to rebel activity. He was nice enough, and pretty average. He often offered to referee our baseball games when he saw us heading to the small grassy field near the school. When he was a kid growing up in Havana, he'd told us, he used to be the best pitcher on his street, but he messed up his throwing hand doing fisherman's work for his father. We always turned him down. We saw him hanging out a lot with the police officers on their lunch breaks, but we'd heard enough stories about kids being found dead in the streets, and Mami had told me to be careful about strangers.

It seemed to Señor Moreno, on that night, that Rafi Consuelo and the man were arguing, because he saw them waving their hands around a lot. Despite how far away they were, he could still hear a faint sliver of their voices floating out into the open air. He didn't hear what they'd said, but he could tell they were talking, and they were angry. Eventually, the man persuaded Rafi Consuelo to get into his big black shiny car, and off they went speeding into the darkness.

Señor Moreno didn't think much of it until Rafi Consuelo didn't come back the next day. Or the next. Or the day after that.

His house was dim and barren, all the lights off. Every time someone from the neighborhood walked by, they craned their heads and tried peeking into the windows.

Everyone had their theories. Pingüino said he'd been abducted by a mobster because he owed him money, and now he was as good as dead. Miguel said he was off getting laid somewhere, the lucky bastard, but I didn't think so. Papi thought rebels as usual. Abuelo didn't know and didn't care. He said he wasn't even sure how Rafi Consuelo had gotten onto our street in the first place: How does a student with no money, no parents or relatives to speak of, end up living in a house on his own? There was something suspicious about that, Abuelo thought. As for me, I didn't like guessing.

No one dared mention the police until the second person went missing. Anita Valle, another former University of Havana student, also in her twenties. It had been rumored Anita was an old girlfriend of Rafi Consuelo's back when they'd been at the University together. She was a pretty, flat-chested black girl who'd babysat me and Pingüino a few years ago. All she did was spend her time flipping through the channels, because she'd never seen a television before. It wasn't even like she was watching anything.

She just liked sitting on the ground in front of the screen and turning the knob, letting the different images wash the light onto her face. She was also an amazing cook, although not as good as Mami. She could throw together *arroz con pollo* faster than anyone I knew.

There were no witnesses the night she disappeared. The only person who said he'd seen anything was her little brother, Diego, who was ten, the same age as Pingüino. He said he'd been half-asleep when he saw it, but he swore he knew it was her – his older sister Anita Valle sneaking out of her room in the middle of the night, fully clothed. And a few seconds later the hinges on the door creaking, closed shut in a way that made him think she was trying to be quiet.

Gone. Just like Rafi Consuelo in the middle of the night. And no witnesses. Not one.

The whispers in the middle of the night. Papi and Mami in the kitchen and me hunched outside the doorway, watching their shadows move on the floor.

What if it's Batista? That car – what if it was the police? What if there's a rat? But that's crazy. Maybe in Havana or Oriente. But not here. Not our street. Not Marianao. Please not Marianao, don't let there be a rat here, please not here…

Tío Rodrigo had informed the police of both disappearances, but he told us there was nothing he could do. The police had told him not to worry. He told us to keep quiet, to not panic, to keep the peace. But in the middle of the night whispers, I heard Mami, the trepidation in her voice.

*¿Y Rodrigo?…* You don't think…?

# 4 La Mañana Después

It was morning and I walked into the living room. Papi was tangled in a bundle of blankets on the couch. Mami stood over him, livid.

"Where were you?" she said.

"I told you, Deianeira, I had to work."

"Don't give me that shit. Miguel almost blown up at the Hotel, Carmen over here in hysterics, and there I was half scared to death. Where were you?"

"Papi?"

Mami saw me and turned away. Papi attempted a smile.

"*Hola* Dela," Papi said. "Are you ready for school?"

"Yes. But Pingüino's still sleeping."

"Adela, get your brother up, please," Mami said, "I'm walking you to school today."

"You are?"

"*Sí, mija.* So get moving."

Ten minutes later and we were walking out into the humidity. Outside, Señor Moreno sat on his front steps reading the newspaper and a few dogs snaked in and out of the allamanda bush of yellow flowers that separated Rafi Consuelo's house and Señor Moreno's. He waved when he saw us and we waved back. The roads were cracked, speckled, and gravelly and the power lines sagged with the palms. The sidewalks were so battered and broken-up in places that it was easier to walk in the gutter or on the street or on a wayward patch of grass. On the parts of the street where the jungle ran wild alongside it, there were bits and pieces of garbage like tires and stray shoes. The Valles' house was almost as lifeless as Rafi Consuelo's, and I saw Mami watching it and its drawn shutters as we passed it by. Mami was wearing her faded flower print dress, the yellow one she wore when she didn't feel like thinking about what to wear. It was ugly and smelled of oldness and no one knew where it came from.

"Stand up straight," Mami told me, "You look like an old man."

Mami used to be a dancer. She loved ballet and every once in a while, when Papi happened to have a little money lying around, he took her to the theatre in Havana to see *Swan Lake*. I loved it when that happened because I loved watching her get ready. It was the only time she sat at the old dressing table that had belonged to my grandmother.

She'd sit there for hours with all the brushes and the paints. She'd dab them on like an artist in front of the mirror, which was ornate and silver and so glamorous it could have belonged in a palace in France. I was fascinated by her lipstick especially, red and shining and sometimes sticking to her teeth when she didn't notice, but I loved it anyway.

"Mami, I don't want to go to school," Pingüino said all of a sudden. "The nuns are mean and boring. Diego's cousin, Armando, doesn't go to school and he's just fine."

"Diego's family is poor and black and it's a miracle they can read, much less that they could afford sending Anita Valle to college. You should be grateful. *Cállate, mijo.*"

"*Pero Mami —*"

"*Dios mío, qué mucho tu jodes,*" Mami threw her hands in the air. "Why don't you talk about something else?"

Pingüino knew better than to talk back. We walked in silence a while before I asked the question I'd been thinking about since I saw Papi on the couch in the bundle of blankets.

"Where was Papi last night?"

Mami pretended like she hadn't heard. Pingüino adjusted his bag as he walked.

"Mami, where do you think –?"

"*Oye*, it's Luis," Mami said, "*Hola* Luis!"

Luis Rodriguez stood on the other side of the street. Luis was the son of an old family friend, Señora Rodriguez. He resembled her a bit around the eyes. He had that old soul look, the kind that made you think he was wise beyond his years. Like Rafi and Anita, he was only in his twenties and used to be a student at the University of Havana. But he wasn't very handsome. His ears stuck out too much, he had an awkward black mustache, and he seemed perpetually nervous, adjusting his glasses to make sure they weren't slipping. His shirt was a battlefield of old stains and he wore khakis that hadn't been washed in a few days.

"*Hola* Señora Santiago," Luis said.

"Luis, I thought you were away."

"I came back early. Where's Rafi?"

"Didn't you hear?"

"Hear? About what?"

"Rafi's gone."

"Gone?"

"Disappeared. A car took him away in the middle of the night. Anita's gone too."

"What?" Luis's face had gone pale, like he'd eaten a bad *arroz con leche*.

"Your mother didn't tell you?"

"I just got back. What about the police? Do they know anything?"

"There's been no news yet. But you know how they are."

"Yes, but what do they know already?"

"Rafi was picked up and Anita snuck out, but they think she was taken too. And that's it."

"Can you excuse me a moment? I need to go."

Luis's eyes were shifting, panicky, like those of the dog who'd been run over two years ago near the house. It had happened overnight. A taxi filled with drunken tourists heading back from the cabaret had run over one of the stray dogs on our street. We woke up to the whimpering and the yowling the next morning, the dog lying with its ribs crushed at the foot of Abuelo's car near our house. I remember Miguel, Pingüino, and I standing over the body, Pingüino wondering if he should touch it, and the dog's eyes rolling and flashing, like someone flipping the channels on the television too fast.

Mami was perturbed. "Well, if you ever need to talk, Luis, you can come to us."

"*Sí. Buenos días.*" He stumbled off. We walked on. I glanced back once to watch him, and he eyed the street before sneaking into his own house, two houses down from our own. A small coral house with a pristine white rocking chair in the front, fit for an American grandmother, and a clump of lemon trees in the back.

Pingüino giggled. "He was drunk as hell."

Mami smacked Pingüino in the arm.

"*¡Ay!* What was that for?"

"Watch your language, Pingüino, I mean it."

"What? But I didn't even –!"

Mami sighed and gazed up toward the sky as if asking God for patience. But it was more than frustration. For a moment I thought I saw sadness. Like when a breeze went by and the petals of a flower moved so limply they seemed defeated. But like always, it melted away when she thought someone was watching. She smiled in a faltering way.

"I think you two can make it from here on your own." She kissed us both on the foreheads before leaving, waving good-bye at the corner where we could no longer see her, her tired yellow dress fluttering limply in the breeze.

# 5 Con la Mano Derecha

Sister Tula was one of those nuns that liked the rulers. It was a long one and the wood left red marks an inch wide on the wrists. It bent before it hit, then snapped – *smack-smack-smack*. The whole class winced.

I didn't get the ruler much, but the girl next to me, Maria Viramontes, got it all the time. She was left-handed, which was a problem, because according to Sister Tula, "All God's children use their right hands." Maria was a nice girl with a pretty, round face, but she cried easily. When the tears started streaming and her face went red, Sister Tula got even madder. "*¿Eres estúpida o qué?*" And she'd smack her again.

We didn't learn much in school. We wore uniforms and socks that itched at our ankles. We sat at our desks and sweltered in the heat as the teacher wrote Bible verses on the board. We tried not to drop things on the floor while Sister Tula was speaking, because then she might get angry and hit us with the ruler.

When Sister Tula got to talking about God, it was easy to get bored. Sometimes she talked for an hour and I became fixated on the palm tree that drooped by the window. If it was nice outside, the fronds swayed a little and you could hear the whoosh of it through the walls. But if it was raining, you could see the raindrops plunking onto the leaves.

There were also the mornings when we "prayed for penance." An hour a day, kneeling on rice grains, praying to God to forgive us for our sins. The rice was oblong and hard and embedded itself into our skin. By the end of it, there were dots on the underside of our knees and rice grains sticking like ticks to our legs. When it was time to go to class, the rice grains detached and made a trail down the hallway.

It was raining today and we were writing paragraphs about José Martí, a Cuban revolutionary who fought against Spain and got himself shot on the first day of battle. I didn't like him very much. The picture of him in the textbook reminded me of Luis Rodriguez because of his stuck-up ears and black mustache. Except José Martí was even uglier – he was skinny as a scarecrow and his hairline stopped way at the top of his head and his mustache was so big it was like a giant furry butterfly had landed on his lips. The things he wrote were nice, but they were the expected things about liberty and fighting for what you believed in. It was hard imagining him starting a revolution or leading troops into battle. I was thinking about José Martí's mustache and how it might fit onto Pingüino's face when Sister Tula's voice interrupted.

"Maria, how many times have I told you? You write *con la mano derecha.*"

*Smack-smack-smack.*

Maria cried by the teacher's desk. Sister Tula glowered from behind her glasses. Maria mumbled something and her voice was fogged over with tears.

"What was that? What did you say? Speak up." The ruler wavered in Sister Tula's hands.

"I – I said that José Martí was left-handed."

"What?"

"My Papi told me I was different because I was left-handed, and that José Martí was different too."

I figured Maria would get smacked again because that was what usually happened. Instead, Sister Tula was bewildered a moment before she said, "Back to your seat." The class watched in astonishment as Maria was set free. She walked to her desk, eyes on the floor. Her hair hung and covered her face. As she settled into the seat next to me, I heard her trying to sob in a way that was quiet.

Outside, the palm tree was drooping.

The rain plunked and the leaves shuddered behind her.

## 6 Con la Mano Izquierda

Abuelo's car smelled like cigars, whiskey, and *agua de coco*. It was a blue the color of hard candy and if you squinted a little, it could've been a gangster car. It was mostly Papi that drove it into Havana to work at the shoe shop, but we called it Abuelo's car because Abuelo was too stubborn to think of it any other away. He won it off a guy – *un italiano* – in the casino long before I was born and it had been his ever since. For all I knew, it could've been nice before, but these days, it was old and battered and the wheels were rusted like old bicycles that had been left out in the rain. Whiskey with *agua de coco* was Abuelo's favorite drink and whenever he decided to go for a drive, it was Pingüino who was stuck making it for him. That rarely happened, but even so, there was still an empty cup in the front seat next to Papi and it smelled of alcohol.

As we drove into Havana, I gazed out the windows, at the chaos of it all. What I loved about it most were the people. There were old ladies smoking cigars on the sidewalk and girls with their skirts cinched who giggled at the young men. In the streets, the old men peered over the balconies at the boys Pingüino's age who played baseball with their shirts off.

And the buildings, of course – I'd never been to Spain, but that must be what it was like. The cathedrals, the castles, el Malecón by the sea. In the older part of the city where Papi worked, the buildings were crumbly and beautiful. Some had huge red domes and others were colonial houses with large glinting windows. The streets were lined with rugged cobblestone and dirt-specked buildings that popped with color every few blocks –

tangerine, bright turquoise, pink, lizard green. Alleyways turned into staircases with shops on the side, their signs hanging over the streets in mid-air. In the newer part, the buildings were different. They were white and tall like pillars of salt in the sun. The streets were filled with people and fancy cars and bicyclists with fresh produce in their baskets and vendors at the stoplights who sold guavas, *guapén*, mangoes, *plátanos*, water bottles, and miniature Cuban flags.

The tanks were leaving the city as we drove in and we had to stop at an intersection as one of them rolled by, huge and green, the cannon sticking out like an eyestalk. Pingüino had never seen a tank in person and he was fascinated, staring with his mouth agape, nudging me and saying, "It's so *big*, Adela." When the tank passed, we drove on. Traffic in Havana was never-ending and we drove with the windows down so that the honking drifted in, the vague curse words lazing about in the air.

I was leery about being in the car with Papi. The last time he'd driven us to the shoe shop, he kept bothering Pingüino about the nine-year-old girl in his class named Lucía and saying that he'd seen Pingüino making goo-goo eyes at her in church and that he had asked Mami to organize the wedding already. Pingüino kept hitting him on the shoulder every time he said something stupid, but Pingüino laughed anyway because Papi could make things funny even when they weren't. Until we stopped at an intersection and there was a girl with a short skirt and high heels walking at the curb. It was obvious she was a prostitute. You saw them more in the alleyways in groups, but rarely alone. She was thin, but her shirt was up to her navel and her skin hung out a bit at the back. Then the light turned green and Papi and Pingüino were laughing about girls and Papi said, "Hey, look at this one." He rolled down the window and yelled "*¡PUTA!*" as he drove around the corner. It was only a split second, but I would never forget the expression on the girl's face as she spun around to see who had called her a whore. It was the same as Maria's when Sister Tula smacked her in the front of the classroom. In the end, she was a girl just like me and Lucía and poor Maria Viramontes. I knew she was a prostitute, but I couldn't help but feel sorry for her anyway. For a while afterwards it was hard seeing Papi, the same man who had taught me to ride a bike and to write my name in cursive, without seeing the girl's face and the slight 'o' of her mouth and the question in her eyes as he raced away from her roaring with laughter.

"Listen," Papi said from the front seat. "I'm taking you both to work because Mami is helping Señora Rodriguez with something. You know the rules. If a customer comes in, be respectful and then come and get me or Dulce."

Me and Pingüino nodded. Papi ran a hand through his hair. "I heard about the bombing."

"Oh," Pingüino said.

"Are you both okay?"

"Yes," I said.

Pingüino fiddled with his fingers, tapped them on his knees, because Pingüino could never keep still.

"Papi," I said. "Was José Martí left-handed?"

"I don't know. Why?"

"Because Maria got smacked with the ruler for writing with her left hand, and she said José Martí was different and left-handed."

"Different, maybe, but I don't know about left-handed. This girl got smacked for that?"

"Sister Tula says God's children only use their right hands."

Papi shook his head in the mirror. "*Qué mierda.* What shit."

"I don't get it," I said. "Was she saying José Martí was bad?"

"What do you mean?"

"He died on the first day of fighting. He failed."

"That doesn't make him bad, it makes him imperfect. And José Martí didn't fail."

"Yes he did, he—"

"I don't like José Martí," Pingüino said. "His head is a weird shape. And so is his mustache."

"He looks like Luis Rodriguez," I said.

Pingüino laughed and Papi sighed. "You both should have more respect. José Martí was a deep thinker and a great poet."

Pingüino wrinkled his nose. "What?"

"You read poetry?" I said.

"Ew," Pingüino said.

"I read his. Don't you know *Cultivo una rosa blanca?*"

"Is that part of *Guantanamera?*" I asked.

"A part of it is, but... You really haven't heard it?" We stared at him through the rearview mirror. Papi cleared his throat:

"I grow a white rose,
in July as in January,
for the sincere friend who
gives me his honest hand.

And for the cruel one who tears
from me the heart with which I live,
thorn nor thistle do I grow;
I grow the white rose."

"...But what does that mean?" Pingüino said.

"Think about it," Papi said.

"I get it, I think. But I don't understand," I said.

"That's okay, Dela," Papi said, gazing out the side window. "White roses are hard sometimes."

His head became very still, so still it might have been made of wax. Even the droplets on the front window moved more than he did. Out the side window there was a little boy, hardly older than Pingüino, with his ribs sticking skinny from his bare chest like a washboard. His face was smeared with dirt and he sat at the curb with bare feet, watching our car go by. It was like he'd been sitting there for ages, waiting for our car. The top of his shirt was wet from the recent rain. It wasn't long before he disappeared in the blur of dirty buildings, and the occasional weed sticking up defiantly from the ground. Then the whiteness of the Havana buildings took his place, as if the ugliness had never existed.

Papi put his eyes back on the road. "White roses are hard for me too."

The shoe shop in Old Havana was run-down and ugly-looking on the outside. The paint was green and peeling from the walls and the golden letters of Zapatería de Cuba were fading into dust. That wasn't to say the inside wasn't run-down and ugly-looking too. Papi tended to be disorganized, so his workbench in the back was strewn with old shoes and bits of people's soles and loose shoelaces. Lining the walls were boxes and boxes of shoes – loafers and solid-colored high heels and old lady sandals made of leather. The whole place reeked of it, really. Walking in was one long, warm gust of leather.

Papi inherited the business from Abuelo. He was never meant to run the shop, but when Mami got pregnant with me in college, there wasn't much else to be done. At the time, he was studying to become a lawyer and Mami was studying to be a nurse like Abuela Adela, but then both of them dropped out. I'm not sure if Abuelo ever approved, but I know he wished Mami had finished school. When we were sitting together in the living room watching the black-and-white TV, he would say, "All that money I saved to put her through college, the least she could do is finish." That was what Abuelo did most of the day – complain. And when he wasn't complaining about some ache or pain, he was sitting on the couch watching television or listening to *Radio Reloj*, the local radio station.

The shoe shop was the reason Papi took Abuelo's car every day. He didn't make enough money for us to maintain the car and to pay tuition for Catholic school and to have a black-and-white

TV and a whole other list of things. Most of our money came from the plantation, and a distant uncle of Papi's in America who was a lawyer. Papi didn't like his uncle, I could tell, because every time he got an envelope filled with cash, he'd stare at it with such hatred, I wondered why he even took his money at all.

He would never tell me why he hated his uncle so much, but I assumed it was because he was an American. Papi really hated them. He ranted about them every day, about how they were the reason for the drugs, and the prostitutes, and the casinos. They were the reason Havana was dangerous, the reason for the poverty. If you walked a little ways down the street, you saw the kids on the sidewalks and their mothers with their skirts stained. And it was all the Americans' fault, according to Papi. We were lucky, he said. Very lucky. But the truth was I didn't need him to tell me those things. It didn't take much to remind you how lucky you were.

When we walked in, there was that gust of leather air in our faces and Dulce at her desk. As far as I knew you didn't particularly need a receptionist to run a shoe shop, but I guess Dulce could be helpful sometimes. Mostly she sat there and looked bored, but every once in a while she would get a terrific spurt of energy and organize the place. You'd walk in and it would be unrecognizable – Papi's trinkets and things on the workbench organized into sections, and the boxes clean and dusted and perfectly arranged by size and whether they were men's, women's, or children's. And Dulce would be standing on a chair trying to get the duster on the very tippy-top shelf with her tongue sticking out.

There was a customer talking to Dulce at her desk, and when Papi saw her, he stiffened. She was skinny and dark-skinned, like she was part black for sure, and she had on a tight, knee-length skirt with a slit that left her legs exposed to the open air. They were pretty girl legs, but sweating slightly because it was hot in the shoe shop and we only had the one fan. She had a pair of old red shoes in her hands and they were flamenco shoes. On the desk was the box where she'd gotten them from, and the tissue paper was unfurled across the surface. I realized I'd seen her before hanging around the shop, but I couldn't pinpoint when or what her name was. She wore lipstick, like Mami when she was going out, except it wasn't as nice somehow. And she had lots of eye makeup, clunky and bristly on her eyelashes. Her top was worn and fuzzy, and it went off her shoulders. I also noticed she had a beauty mark above her upper lip, like singers on the television.

"How much?" she asked Dulce about the shoes.

"*Treinta*," Dulce said, and the girl sighed.

"It's too bad. They're beautiful and I want them."

"They're a bit old though, don't you think? And they're dirty too."

"I still want them."

"Yes, well you can't have them…" Dulce turned from her. "*Hola* Señor Santiago. *Hola* Pingüino. *Hola* Adela. ¿*Qué pasa chica?*"

"*Nada.*"

"And you, Pingüino? How was school?"

"Fine," Pingüino said sullenly.

"This is my sister Celia," Dulce said, introducing the girl. "She'll be leaving soon."

"Are you the shop owner?" Celia asked Papi.

"Yes," Papi said.

"Is there any way I can get these shoes for a lesser price? I really do want them."

"No, I'm sorry. I could perhaps find you something similar in the back."

"But I don't want something similar. I want these."

"Celia!" Dulce hissed.

"Well, I do," Celia said, "Is it so shameful to want something and not be able to have it? But that's just the way with things. Isn't it, Señor Santiago?"

"I – I suppose so."

"That's enough, Celia," Dulce said. "Why are you here? It's not the shoes, it never is."

"What's that supposed to mean?"

"There's always more. You never show up without there being more."

"You think I want money, don't you?"

Dulce's eyes flicked towards Papi. "I never said that, I just think –"

Celia shoved the shoes back into the box with the tissue paper and there was a sound of crumpling. We watched without speaking. She marched back to the mish-mash of what may have been, at some point, the women's section, and placed the box on top of a mountain of mismatched Mary Janes.

"Maybe I don't need them," she said. "Maybe I can learn to not have them, or... Can I talk to you?"

"Me?" Papi said.

"Him?" Dulce said.

"Yes, him."

Papi saw me and Pingüino standing there with our school stuff weighing us down, and didn't know what to do.

"Why don't the both of you do your homework in the back?"

Me and Pingüino stared at him. The one thing Papi never did was ask us to do our homework. Pingüino shrugged, "Okay." He shuffled away.

As I walked by, I attempted to pick out Dulce's features in Celia's face other than the skin color. There wasn't much resemblance, except for maybe the nose, which was wide and glistening. She met my eyes and I felt embarrassed for having stared at her, but I was struck by how desperate she was about her red shoes and her need to want them. I was almost to the back door when I heard Papi whisper something: "You need to leave. We'll talk later." Celia was about to protest, but Papi forced her out the door. Celia stumbled and caught herself. She walked away and glanced at Papi once through the window before melding into the hustle and bustle of the sidewalk. Before I knew it, she was gone.

When we got home, Miguel was waiting for us on the front porch. He did that after work because he didn't have many friends apart from a janitor at the Hotel Nacional named Julio – and him he'd only mentioned once in passing. Miguel was taller than most sixteen-year-olds, and his limbs were as skinny as a stickman's. He was a few shades darker than the rest of us, a caramel color I was jealous of. He claimed to hate his job at the Hotel Nacional because of all the gringos he had to deal with, but I think he secretly loved the glamor of it all. I didn't blame him. Even though I knew the place was crawling with Americans, there were times when I dreamt of the big pool in the back and thought of what it must feel like to float in chlorine instead of saltwater. Me and Pingüino loved asking about what went on inside that mysterious building in Vedado. Large and towering compared to everything around it, its white walls and red roofs gleamed in the sunshine and rows of palm trees lined the road with the rich people's cars and taxis.

I remember once long before the bombing when we sat on the front porch and listened to Miguel talk about the Hotel. Los americanos that came to the Hotel Nacional, he said, were all the color of milk and had skinny butts and fancy bags made of leather. The pool was a giant concrete bathtub that people scraped their toes against if they weren't careful, and the water had so much chlorine it made people's hair squeak when they got out afterwards. The color was blue. Kind of like the shallow part of the sea, but less greenish. It was more fake, more glow-in-the-dark. But those American women, Miguel said. *Coño*, were they cute. Their bathing suits were cut perfect for their bodies and they were always trying to get their milk-skin to bronze. But all that happened was their cheeks got too pink like undercooked meat.

Then I remember Pingüino asked about the mobsters and whether or not they kept their guns with them at the pool. Miguel said no, but they were really macho, really scary. They kept their girls nearby and smoked so many cigars that the ashtrays were strewn with burnt logs like a forest had burned to the ground. And they wore these gold chains around their necks... in the *pool – en la piscina*.

Miguel hadn't talked to us about the Hotel since then, except once to say that Julio had broken his foot falling down the stairs after slipping on a puddle of water. Today, Miguel was seated on the second step of the porch, one leg dangling out in front of him, and we were gathered around him like schoolchildren. Miguel yanked a sprig of grass from the ground and twirled it around his fingers.

Pingüino berated him with questions. "Does Tío know who planted the bomb?"

"No."

"How loud was it, do you think?"

"Well, I couldn't hear for a while afterwards."

"Did anybody die?"

"No, *estúpido*. It was in the papers. No one was injured."

"Was it cool, like in a movie?"

"Depends what you mean by cool."

"Were you scared? Did you cry?"

Miguel quit twirling the piece of grass in his hands. "Well –"

"I bet you cried, didn't you? Are you –?"

"*Dios mío*, Pingüino, let him breathe," I said.

Miguel shrugged, and let the piece of grass fall to the ground. "It's fine."

"So is everything all right at the Hotel now?" I asked.

"The bomb didn't do much. The shrapnel went into some of the palm trees and there was a piece in my backpack, but that was it. It didn't land near anything important... I mean, except me."

"But you did cry, though, didn't you?" Pingüino asked.

"No, Pingüino, I didn't cry!" Miguel yelled. "Although I'm sure you would've, you little wuss."

"I am not a wuss. And I bet you did cry, but you're too chicken to admit it. You're scared even now."

Miguel tried laughing it off, but it didn't work. I thought of the dry trail of tears down his cheeks the night before.

"Everyone's scared, Pingüino," I said. "Especially with what's happened to Rafi and Anita."

Pingüino scoffed. "I'm not scared. I went over to Rafi Consuelo's house just the other day, and there was nothing to be afraid of."

"Yes, there was. Mami if she caught you."

I explained to Miguel about the letter Pingüino's school had sent home because of what Pingüino had done with the lizards and Miguel laughed. Pingüino crossed his arms. "Like you're not scared either, Adela. You can't even walk by Rafi Consuelo's house without trembling. Don't pretend like I haven't seen you."

"That's because I'm not stupid. Like you."

Pingüino stuck his tongue out at me and I ignored him. "Are you still going to work there?" I asked Miguel.

"My mom wants me to quit, but I like having my own money. Mind you, I was half-tempted today. There was this big fat tomato of a gringo in the restaurant with his big fat tomato family saying things about how *wonderful* the beach was and how *wonderful* the food was if only the people everywhere weren't poor and making things ugly."

"*Los americanos son extraños*," I said. "The Americans are strange. Papi says it's all their fault. Maybe they don't know it yet."

The screen door opened and Papi walked shirtless out of the house, "Miguel, it's almost six o'clock. You should probably head home. Your mother will be worried."

"Sure thing, Tío. No problem."

"How are you doing?"

"I'm fine."

"Good. Now, go home before your mother has another breakdown."

"*Adiós, primos*," Miguel said.

"Goodbye, Miguel," we said

Miguel walked down the street and disappeared at the corner.

Papi gazed at us before walking in. We followed him, and I thought about *los americanos*. I thought about the ones Miguel had mentioned with the luggage made of leather. I thought about the women that sunned themselves by the pool and the big fat tomato gringo with his big fat tomato family. I wondered if they knew about everything. About the poverty and the torture and the fact that most people couldn't read. But perhaps it was hard knowing something was your fault if you were cocooned inside the Hotel Nacional with its concrete-bathtub pool and its palm-tree-lined roadways and its tall red roofs. Perhaps that was the world to them. Perhaps they would never know my world and I would never know theirs. Perhaps it was better that way.

Sometimes, if we knocked on her front door and said *por favor*, she let me and Pingüino pick lemons from the trees that grew scraggly in her backyard. Which was exactly what we did on Saturday morning. Luckily, it wasn't raining and she let us in. Mami said that Señora Rodriguez was only forty, but she didn't seem that way. She was like an *abuela* with wrinkles around her eyes and mouth. When she smiled, her teeth were pearly and you could almost imagine she was beautiful once.

Me and Pingüino, we came prepared.

We armed ourselves with the white bucket Mami used to clean the floors and long-sleeved shirts for leaning deep into the branches. Señora Rodriguez's lemon trees grew along the back fence and were wild and crazed. The lemons weren't ready so most of them were green, except for those few that grew yellow and plump way in the back. Because Pingüino was so little, I had to hold onto the back of his shirt when he leaned in to grab one. It was slow and hot and soon there were sweat stains on the pits of our lemon-picking shirts.

"Hey, Pingüino," I said as I held him by the shirt.

"Mmm-hmm?"

"Where's Luis?"

"Does it matter?"

"I don't know. I was just wondering."

"Well then, don't mention it. Can't you see I'm concentrating here? *¡Carajo!*" The lemon he'd been pulling at ripped free and plummeted through the brambles. It fell to an indiscernible part of ground, most likely near the fence.

"Pingüino!"

"Sorry."

"That's the fifth one! *¡Mira lo que estás haciendo, cabrón!*"

"You keep distracting me. And don't curse. Do you want Señora Rodriguez to hear?"

I readjusted my grip. My hands were sweaty and my fingers hurt. "You cursed just now."

"I'm not anymore." He quieted down as he set his sights on another lemon, this one fatter than the last. It was closer than the other one had been, but we'd missed it because it was curtained in a tangle of leaves and thin, scratchy branches. It was so close I saw the pores on its skin.

"Ooh. Get that one. That one's good."

"*Shhht.*"

He leaned forward. My fingers tightened on his shirt. A drop of sweat tickled my brow. I wiped it away. All was silence, save for the sound of Pingüino's shoes crunching through the dead leaves at the fringe of the lemon trees. He reached his arm through the gaps in the tangle of branches. His fingers brushed the bright yellow peel and I had a sudden thought.

"Hey, Pingüino," I said before I could stop myself.

Pingüino jumped and the humongous lemon he had just plucked fumbled from his fingers. It made a ruckus as it smashed to the ground and rolled to the back where, once again, we could not reach.

"*¡ME-CAGO-EN-LA-PUTA-MADRE-QUE-TE-PARIO-PERRA-CABRONA!*" he screamed.

The back door of Señora Rodriguez's coral house swung open and Señora Rodriguez stood in the doorway, smoking a cigarette in a pink nightgown and bare feet. I let go of Pingüino. He lost his balance and almost crashed into the lemon trees.

"*Niños.* I hope I didn't hear what I think I heard."

"It was Adela, Señora Rodriguez," Pingüino said. My jaw dropped.

Señora Rodriguez sighed. "I don't doubt it. Most children curse when their parents aren't listening. At least when they think they aren't listening."

Señora Rodriguez took another drag of her cigarette before waving the smoke at us. "Hurry up and pick those lemons so I can squeeze them. That's what you came for, isn't it?"

We nodded.

When we had filled up a third of the bucket, Señora Rodriguez made her lemonade, which was better even than Abuelo's. Me and Pingüino sat at the counter in front of the fan, elbowing each other for room. Señora Rodriguez's kitchen was small and rickety, a thin streak of rust lining the spot where the sink ended and the blue-and-white wallpaper began. As I watched Señora Rodriguez press the lemon husks into the juicer with her hands wrinkled like an *abuela*'s, I thought of Luis again.

"Señora Rodriguez, where's Luis?"

"What?" she said, not taking her eyes off the juicer.

"Luis. Where is he?"

"I don't know." She sighed as she threw a shriveled lemon husk into the sink. "I hardly know what that boy does anymore."

The fringes of Señora Rodriguez's pink nightgown were frayed and there were burn marks on the skirt. If I concentrated, I could see the crests of her nipples poking through. I didn't think Señora Rodriguez ever wore a bra and I wondered if she had ever worn a bra, even when she was young. I wondered if I would need a bra soon. I hoped so. I didn't want to end up flat-chested like Anita Valle had been. I wasn't sure why being flat-chested was such a bad thing, but from the way Miguel talked, if I didn't want to end up dying alone, I probably should pray for some breasts.

The front door opened.

"Luis, is that you?"

"*Sí, Mamá.*" He walked into the kitchen and his ears stuck out as prominently as ever. He really did look like José Martí.

"Oh good. I was just making some lemonade for Adela and Pingüino. Do you want any?"

"Adela and Pingüino?"

"Yes. The two Santiago kids."

He blinked as if he didn't recognize us. "Two of them?"

"Yes. There's another one. Their cousin Miguel, remember? You used to play with him when you were little."

"Oh."

"Are you okay, *corazón?*"

"Yes, *Mamá*... I –" Luis took an uncertain step forward. He was about to say something and changed his mind. He stepped back. "...I'm sorry."

He rushed down the hallway and I was surprised at how fast Señora Rodriguez went after him.

"Luis, come back."

"*No, Mamá.*"

"At least have some lemonade."

"*No, Mamá.* I don't want any."

The door slammed as Luis retreated to his room. Señora Rodriguez screamed. "If you won't tell me what's wrong, at least tell me what I can do to help. Luis? Luis?"

We waited for the silence to end, to hear Señora Rodriguez's muffled footsteps come back down the hall, to have her pour the lemonade and pretend as if nothing had happened. Instead, we heard the sound of stifled sobs, quiet and gasping. I got up from the stool, the legs scraping loudly against the floor, and Pingüino followed. We found Señora Rodriguez crying in the hallway, hugging herself so hard she made finger marks on her own arms. She sat on the ground, her knees drawn up to her chest, not caring if her underwear showed.

"Señora Rodriguez?" Pingüino asked. "Are you okay?"

Señora Rodriguez sniffled and wiped her nose with her hand. "Of course I'm okay. I'm always okay. Adults are supposed to be okay, aren't they? Maybe you two should go now."

"What about the lemonade?" Pingüino asked.

I stomped on his foot.

"*¡Ay!*"

"What's wrong with you?" I hissed.

"No, it's all right," Señora Rodriguez said, blowing hair out of her face. She picked herself off the ground and wiped the tears from her cheeks. "I promised lemonade, and lemonade I will give."

We stayed as silent as we could as she finished pressing the husks into the juicer, flinching every time she was done with a lemon and threw it into the sink with a loud bang. By the end of it, lemon juice had squirted onto the ceiling, onto the linoleum, onto the blue-and-white of the wallpaper. She gave a shuddery breath as she poured the lemon juice into two glasses along with some water and sugar. She mixed it with two silver spoons so old they had speckles on the hilt. I didn't complain.

"Run along," she said as she gave it to us, spoons and all. I watched the bits of translucent pulp settle to the bottom. "Bring back the cups and spoons the next time you're over here."

"Yes, Señora Rodriguez. We will. I hope you feel better," I said, before she could usher us out the door.

She nodded. Her nightgown had lemon juice on it, right over her left nipple. I pretended not to notice.

The walls were the color of oranges and when the sun came up, it was blinding. Mami and Papi didn't have much money when they first moved in, but Mami had made sure the kitchen was one of the rooms painted because she'd known it would be where she'd be spending the most time with the garlic cloves, the bags of white rice, the tins of olive oil in the pantry.

Mami loved cooking to music. She always put her hair in a ponytail before stretching to turn on the radio next to the refrigerator. When she was happy, it was Celia Cruz and she salsaed by herself as she stirred the *picadillo* in the pan and plopped in the red peppers. When she was sad, she might not cook at all, but Frank Sinatra played as she sat at the stool and leaned her elbows on the table. In the mornings, it was *Radio Reloj* and she smiled as she asked me and Pingüino what we wanted for breakfast.

What I really loved was when she made *ropa vieja*. On Sundays, she woke me up before the sun rose. I tried nudging Pingüino awake too, but he would groan and put a pillow over his head. So it was just me and Mami next to the kitchen sink in the darkness. I helped her shred the beef and the juice stained my fingertips. It was quiet, except for the breeze and birdsong that drifted in through the open window, rustling Mami's hair and mine too. Then, we put the beef in the copper pot with the garlic, the peppers, the onions, the spice, and the olive oil from the tins.

Today, the beef was cold and dank on my skin. Both of us had a plateful and we shredded it in silence as Mami's fingers moved without thinking – slender fingers tanned more on the outside than in. I studied my own and found them pale the whole way around, the way none of my family's fingers were except mine. Mami broke the silence.

"Have I ever told you about the costumes?"

Mami's eyes were at the window. Within them, the moonlight twirled.

"What costumes?"

"The costumes from when I danced."

"No."

"I wish you could have seen them. They were made out of this silk that glowed. We were only ever dressed in white. I never knew why."

I shrugged. "Maybe because it's nicer. Like..." I thought of José Martí and the white roses. "Like white roses."

Mami gazed out the window. "I used to pretend they were wedding dresses. That there were flowers in my hair because I was getting married... That's where my wedding dress came from."

"What?"

"My wedding dress. It was an old ballet costume."

I thought of the wedding picture in the living room, the one I had passed by every morning on the way to school, every night me and Abuelo sat together and watched television. I had never thought to ask about the dress, had presumed it was tucked away in a corner of the house in a big box with a bow on it.

"Why?"

"Your grandmother had sold hers and we couldn't afford a new one."

"Oh."

"Sometimes..." Mami was pained, trying to find the words. Her fingers continued tearing. I believed she would be tearing forever, trying to find the words. "Sometimes... I wish things had turned out differently."

Her words hung heavy in the air. I could see a stray gray hair streaking out above her head. No one spoke, and we continued on, the only sound of strings of meat being ripped apart. We gazed into the blackness, a single house with its lights a faraway square in the dark. Mami tensed beside me. I recognized the sagging front porch, and the bushes on the side, and the windows that had been dead for weeks. I caught my breath.

It was Rafi Consuelo's house.

"Mami."

"I know, Dela, I see it too."

We stared. And just as suddenly as the lights came on, they went out with a finality.

"Mami –"

She let out a breath. "Don't talk about what we've seen, Adela."

"Okay, but –"

"Don't worry about it." She tucked a golden strand behind my ear. "I'll take care of it, *mija*."

We went back to shredding the meat, and I snuck peeks out the window at Rafi Consuelo's house, wondering if anyone had seen the lights too, trying to discern the slightest brightness behind the closed shutters. But there was nothing. Me and Mami were silent. I could feel her watching me every time my eyes wandered to that dead house down the street.

I knew things would proceed as they did most Sundays. We would go to church. Papi would wear his good dress shirt and the shoes he had shined himself that morning. Abuelo and Pingüino would trail behind, grumbling. And the *ropa vieja* would be stewing in the pot all day until we returned, the aroma seeping its way around the house until dinnertime when Mami cracked the lid open.

With the steam billowing and everyone – even Abuelo – gathered around the pot, her eyes would be satisfied. The same way she would have looked, I imagined, if she'd become a nurse like she was supposed to, if it weren't for me.

I didn't like church much, but I didn't say it out loud, especially not at school where Sister Tula could hear. Abuelo hated church the most, which I didn't understand because I thought old people were supposed to be more religious. Abuelo had stopped praying when my grandmother passed away. He said he only prayed nowadays when he thought it was worth it. On our walk to church that morning, I wondered if he had prayed at all for Rafi Consuelo and Anita Valle in the last few weeks. But as much as I wanted to, I couldn't picture Abuelo getting on his knees by his bedside with his head lowered. He didn't seem the type.

The lights of Rafi Consuelo's house were off as we passed it.

"Strange…" I said.

"What's strange?" Pingüino asked. In front of us, Mami slowed down, listening.

I whispered it in Pingüino's ear. "I'll tell you later."

To me, churches were supposed to be tall with arches and towers and a big bell on top someone had to climb a staircase to get to. I wanted my church to have cobblestone on the outside and wide marble steps that would gleam even when it was raining. I wanted one of the old Spanish churches in Havana that I went into once with Papi to light a candle at the foot of the *la Virgen María*. I remembered everything gilded in gold, and paintings of saints, and stained glass that made the floors glow with triangles of color. I remembered the way footsteps echoed, and the ceiling so high it was as if the walls were growing all around us. Like I'd turn away one moment and come back the next and the place would be a whole world taller.

Instead, I got our ratty church in Marianao. It was a cream color on the outside, with flecks of grit on the walls from years of cars splashing puddles onto them. The windows didn't open because the latches were rusted shut and it took two grown men to get them open. So most of the time we had services with the door open, and hoped for a stray breeze because no one had the money to donate an extra fan. It got hot in there quick, and while sitting in the pews, you'd see women who sweat so much they brought their own handkerchiefs to wipe their faces. The only decoration was a simple wooden cross at the front, and the altar with its tablecloth and cheap golden trim. If you got up closer, you could see the thread was loose on one side and sticking up like a stray hair.

Mami, Papi, Pingüino, and I slid into a pew while Abuelo sat at the aisle. In front of us were Tía Carmen and Miguel and every once in a while Tía Carmen stroked Miguel's hair before placing her hand on his shoulder. Señor Moreno sat behind us and I could hear him clearing his throat in that way of his, like he was permanently clogged. On the opposite side of the church, Anita Valle's little brother, Diego, swung his feet and stared at his fingers. His mother and father were huddled next to him. Behind them were Señora Rodriguez and Luis, Luis fidgeting as always. Tío Rodrigo leaned against the back wall with his arms crossed.

Padre Francisco entered from a side door. He was small and portly with wispy gray hair around a bald spot that shone in the heat. Even though I never listened at church, Padre Francisco was very nice and let Pingüino and I come around twice for communion crackers even though he knew we did it only for the food. As for his sermons, I didn't pay attention when he mentioned things from the Bible. When I was little I would try to understand what he said but I never could. I always felt in those moments when he asked us to pray that I was faking it. I was faking believing in God, in Jesus, in saints. They would always be nothing more than decorations on the inside of pretty Spanish churches in Havana. Still, I sometimes so wanted there to be a God, an entity spread across the stars who would reach out a hand and fix everything, rock me to sleep on those nights when I felt so alone I wanted to curl into myself and never wake up. But that was only sometimes and I wasn't sure sometimes was enough.

"'Though our bodies are dying,'" Padre Francisco read from his Bible, "'our spirits are being renewed every day. For our present troubles are small and won't last very long. Yet they produce for us a glory that vastly outweighs them and will last forever. So we don't look at the troubles we can see now; rather, we fix our gaze on things that cannot be seen. For the things we see now will soon be gone, but the things we cannot see will last forever…'"

He stared into the crowd and the crowd stared back at him.

"I have had many of you coming to me, asking where God has gone. What has He done with our children? What has He done with our parents, our brothers, our sisters? Why does He take some and leave others? How can we go on living knowing any one of us could cease our existences in this place? Perhaps some of you have stopped praying or asking questions altogether because God does not answer you back. And perhaps I could stand here before you and flip through the pages of this Bible until I pretended to find the answers. But I will not do that because it is my job to be truthful in the name of God and I will not deceive you. Instead, I will tell the truth and the truth is this: I cannot tell you what will become of us. I cannot tell you what will become of Rafi Consuelo or Anita Valle or their families. I cannot tell you what will happen tomorrow or next week or next year or even within the next decade. But I can tell you that at this moment, right at this very moment where we know not what will happen, God is watching over us. One day at the penultimate moment of our lives, we will look back. We will remember this church in Marianao, and the people who gathered in its pews, and how small we all felt, and how high we had to rise.

And we will be grateful that we did so. So grateful we will want to fall to our knees in gratitude for the strength God gave us. So I ask of you now to bow down in prayer for those who are lost, for those who have been left behind, for those who have been saved."

Mami was tearful and Papi was unreadable. If I leaned forward, I could see Abuelo's fingers gathered in his lap. Pingüino concentrated on a fly that pinged against the ceiling near a cobweb. Everyone bowed their heads, and Pingüino hurried to follow. I closed my eyes, and drowned out the noises – Pingüino shifting next to me, Señor Moreno's resonating cough, Mami's sniffles as she tried not to cry. My neck was warm and there were goosebumps on my arms. I had never wished so hard for anything in my life.

...Please please please let them be alive, let them all be alive. Don't let them be dead. I don't want them to be dead. I want those lights in Rafi Consuelo's house to be Rafi Consuelo and I want Anita back flipping channels on the television and making *arroz con pollo*. I want them back, *Dios, por favor. Devuélvanlos, por favor.* Give them back, please. Thank you for Miguel, I need him, I don't know what I would do if he... Please help us. Please. Help Mami love herself again. Please be real, I want you to be real...

I opened my eyes and glanced around the room, feeling self-conscious as I closed my eyes one more time... And God? Some breasts wouldn't hurt either. Thanks. Amen.

People prayed and their mouths moved as they whispered. It wasn't long before everyone was finished and Padre Francisco resumed the service. I watched the stray golden thread that stuck up from the end of the altar's tablecloth, thinking. Then from behind us, a shadow blocked the sun streaming in from the open door. I turned and so did Pingüino.

Two men I had never seen before. Both young, both tan, and both with wisps of beards. Their clothes were grungy and green and stiff as if they'd been sweat in a long time ago. They slipped into the last pew on the other side of the church. Tío Rodrigo stood by the back wall, and he narrowed his eyes as they walked past him. Mami poked me and Pingüino in the shoulders because she saw we weren't paying attention.

We turned back around. The fly had stopped pinging against the wall. It was caught in the gossamer web, a small black dot writhing. If it had had a voice it would have been screaming.

At the end of the service, Papi, Mami, Abuelo, Señor Moreno, and the Valles filed up to Padre Francisco at the front. The people in the church idled out to the food on the lawn. I watched as Diego Valle took the hand of Lucía from down the street. She swung a rag doll and her eyes gazed wetly upwards as she stumbled by. Tío Rodrigo waited at the end of the aisle for Tía Carmen, and they walked out together. From the other side of the church, I saw her pursing her lips as Miguel and Pingüino lingered by the pews.

"This can't go on any longer," Señor Moreno was saying at the front, "We can't wait for someone else to be kidnapped and the police are useless. We need to do something."

"Don't be stupid. There's nothing we can do," Papi said, and Mami frowned. "That's the way it works."

"I bet it's those rebels," Señor Moreno spat. "Or the police. If you ask me they're all in on it together, trying to make life a living hell. I say we –"

"What?" Papi said. "Protest? Arm ourselves? It's all been done before. It's happening now and it doesn't do anything. There's never anything anyone can do. It's inevitable."

"No, it's not," Mami said. "It's not if you don't make it that way. The trouble is figuring out where to start."

"What are you suggesting?" Señor Moreno said.

"Nothing," Mami said, blinking. "It's much too dangerous anyway."

"Padre Francisco, what do you think?" Abuelo said.

"I think we should let the police handle this," Padre Francisco said, "What will be will be. Besides there is too much we don't know."

"There are people missing," Señor Moreno said, "This can't go on."

"That's what they all say," Papi said darkly.

"I don't care about any of that," Señora Valle said. "I don't care. Padre —" Her voice broke. "I want my daughter back. Even if it's just a body."

They all went quiet. Señor Valle shifted where he stood and there was a sorrow in his eyes. I was shocked by how so without hope they were, how raw it all was. I tried not to imagine Mami and Papi sad that way, wishing my body would show up somewhere, in a ravine, by a roadside, anywhere — as long as they could throw me a funeral.

"You don't know what it's been like, any of you," Señora Valle said. "I've been waking up every day expecting her to be back, and every day I have woken up to silence. It's not that I'm not grateful. I'm grateful for Diego. But what's scaring me — us — is that for every day we wake without her, a little bit of that expectation chips away. The silence is normal now. I — I find myself having trouble remembering her face. It's like there's nothing except this threat she might never come back or, worse, that she could be home any moment, and we won't be there when she is. It's killing us."

I could tell Padre Francisco was melting on the inside. Not because of what she'd said but because of how often he'd heard it, how often he'd stood there and comforted those left behind. Mami and Papi stood blank and serious. Abuelo was quiet, and I watched as he stood two paces behind, studying us as if he knew what all this was about, had been there before in this church, by this altar, pleading to a priest about God snatching people out of other people's lives.

I felt a tug at my wrists. It was Pingüino.

"What?"

He pulled me away to the doors where Miguel leaned against the yellow hinges. Miguel beckoned to the table outside with the drinks, where Luis Rodriguez and the two strangers stood in a circle, deep in conversation. Pingüino tugged at my wrists again. "Come on," he whispered.

"Why?"

"Don't you want to know what they're saying?"

I tiptoed to see Luis through the chink of open door. I saw his brows drawn together and the gravity on the bearded men's faces.

"No," I lied.

Pingüino rolled his eyes. "*Dios mío*, why can't you be fun for once? Let's go."

He led me into the daylight.

Outside the church, the lawn was balding, the ground brown from all the years of lunches in the sun. I'm not sure what most neighborhoods did after church, but in Marianao people ate until their guts were as large as swallowed balloons. On the lawn, there were four long tables laden with food. The tables were really old – Padre Francisco said thirty years at least – and the edges were worn down from bored children digging their utensils into the edges. On top of the tables were pots and pans of *arroz con pollo*, *picadillo*, *plátanos a puñetazos*, and sometimes if Señora Valle was in the mood, she would make ham *croquetas* me and Pingüino fought over.

There weren't *croquetas* today. There hadn't been any since Anita Valle had disappeared.

Everyone swarmed and made something resembling a line. They grabbed the creamy pink plates that belonged to the church and bunches of metal forks, spoons, and knives, which much like those of Señora Rodriguez, were speckled with age. Predictably, Tío Rodrigo had already made his first roundabout. At gatherings, it was Tío Rodrigo who ate the most. He would come around to each table trying to be discreet. And even when he had a tower of chicken legs ready to topple over, he would go on adding more – *picadillo* over the chicken, and then the *plátanos a puñetazos* on top of that. It was disgusting, but it was always something you could count on, like Miguel sucking the bone marrow from chicken bones, or Papi singing *Guantanamera* when he was drunk, or Abuelo with his whiskey and *agua de coco* when he wanted to go for a drive.

Near the stone path, Diego and Lucía fought over the rag doll. It had lost an arm, and now its shoulder was frayed with stuffing. He pushed her to the grass and she wailed. The grass stains on her butt were visible when she ran crying to her mother. Meanwhile, Luis and the strangers argued, Luis holding a forgotten cup of pineapple juice in his hand.

"Follow my lead and act casual," Miguel said. "Don't ruin this, *tontos.*"

Me and Pingüino followed, and I knew deep down what a bad idea this was. The three of us stood in a loose semicircle with our backs to Luis and the two strangers.

Luis was speaking. "– can't believe you did something so stupid."

"Don't yell at us, we didn't know."

"You didn't tell us."

"I didn't tell you because I didn't know when – or if – you were coming back."

"What do we do?"

"I don't want to *do* anything."

"That wasn't part of the plan."

"It doesn't matter."

"How can you say that? Isn't that what we're fighting against? People who don't think we matter?"

"That's not what I meant."

"But he's right. We need to show them we don't knuckle under. That's what it's all for."

"We'd be hurting people. More than we already have."

"Sometimes that's the price that must be paid."

"No, it isn't."

"They deserve it."

"No," Luis sounded desperate. "They don't."

"It was your idea. Isn't this what you wanted?"

"Yes, but I didn't want... I just want things back to normal."

One of them lowered their voices, and I leaned backwards to catch what he said. "Hey, Rodriguez, do you know those kids?"

A hand grabbed my shoulder. They grabbed Miguel and Pingüino too, and they turned us around. They hadn't washed their faces in a while; I could see the sheen of grime on their foreheads and cheeks. They weren't men at all, but boys in their twenties, the same age as Luis. I could smell forest on their clothing and mud that stunk of rotten things.

"What do you think, Luis?"

Luis didn't respond. He was focused on something else. He perspired beneath his glasses. For once, he quit fidgeting.

Tío Rodrigo.

He sat at the corner of a table, his plate faint with streaks of sauce, his chair twisted in our direction. The green tablecloth fluttered at the corners. Tía Carmen sat next to him, and she rummaged in her purse for something, the wrinkles on her forehead worse than ever. Tío Rodrigo twisted something in his hands – a piece of grass, I think – except it had been destroyed by his fingers. Now, it was only a mangled strand of something that might have once been alive, and he played with it mercilessly, his mouth in a thin line.

Luis and the strangers dispersed.

Miguel quivered beneath his father's stare.

After church, it was the three of us on the front porch again.

"I saw the lights on in Rafi Consuelo's house," I said, as soon as Mami, Papi, and Abuelo went inside.

Pingüino's jaw dropped. "What?"

"This morning. Before the sun rose. Me and Mami saw the lights on."

"Are you sure?" Miguel asked. "It could've been another house."

"It was Rafi Consuelo's house. I know it."

"You're lying!" Pingüino said.

"I'm not."

"But…" Pingüino crossed his arms. "That's not fair."

"What?"

"I went there to throw away my letter and nothing happened. All Adela has to do is get up early and she gets to see all the action. Sometimes I think God doesn't like me."

"Don't make fun, Pingüino. This is serious."

"Are you *sure* it was his house?" Miguel asked again.

"*Yes.* Mami saw it too."

"Do you think he's back?" Pingüino said. He snuck a peek at Rafi Consuelo's house, as if he expected the lights to come blazing back on. The house remained soulless. "Maybe we should knock on the door. Just to see."

"No!" I said, too quickly.

"Oh? Who's scared now?"

"I'm not scared, I'm being careful." I glanced at Miguel to make sure he didn't think I was a sissy because he was the only teenager I was friends with, and I didn't want him thinking I was a sissy. He stared at the front step, the one with the loose board.

"Miguel, should we tell Rodrigo?"

"No. Definitely not. God knows what that would... No. You can't. You don't know..."

"What don't I know?"

Pingüino burst out all of a sudden, "Those rebels smelled bad, didn't they, Miguel?"

Miguel regained his composure, "Yes, they did."

"Pingüino, don't let Mami hear you saying things about rebels or she'll think I said something about the lights. She told me not to say anything. Besides you don't know they were rebels for sure."

"But they had beards like in the papers!"

"And if Señor Moreno grew a beard, would that make him a rebel?"

"No... But Adela, they just were! And after that weird thing at Señora Rodriguez's house yesterday, you can't tell me Luis isn't a rebel too."

"What?" Miguel asked.

"We went over yesterday to pick lemons," I said, "and Luis came home while Señora Rodriguez was making lemonade. Things got strange."

So we told Miguel about the lemonade and Luis being awkward and saying sorry and Señora Rodriguez's lone figure in the hallway and how she had pulled herself off the ground and made us lemonade anyway.

"But what was he apologizing for?" Miguel asked.

The screen door whined open. Papi stood on the porch leaning on the wall with his loafers shiny from this morning. There were sweat stains forming at the pits of his dress shirt.

"Pingüino, your mother wants you."

"¿Qué?"

"*Tu madre*. She wants you."

"What for?"

"To clean the trash you left in your room," Mami said, emerging from the hallway, her apron on, faint notes of salsa floating out from the kitchen. "I bet you thought me or Adela would clean it up, but oh no – Not in this lifetime, *señor*. Move your big Cuban butt. *Arranca*."

"*Pero Mami –*"

"Don't '*Pero Mami*' me. Clean your room. Now."

Pingüino faked a yawn and Papi smiled in amusement. Mami glared at Pingüino. "When I get there in ten minutes, I better see you working."

"Okay, okay. Calm down." Pingüino trundled inside and Papi held the door for him.

"Adela, you should come inside too," Mami said, "I want to get Abuelo away from that television screen. I think he's going blind staring at that thing."

Miguel's face was gray.

"Can I have a few more minutes?" I asked.

"Maybe," Mami said. "How was the shoe shop the other day?"

"What?"

"When Papi picked you up from school and took you to the shoe shop."

I shrugged. "It was fine. We met Dulce's sister, Celia."

The floorboards creaked beneath Papi's feet.

"I didn't know Dulce had a sister. What's she like?"

I met Papi's eyes over Mami's shoulder. I couldn't tell if he was shaking his head, or if I was imagining it, if the sun was playing tricks on my eyes like on hot days when the heat made mirages of the sea and the sky in Havana. I remembered Celia and her fuzzy top, the slit along her skirt, the cheap makeup. I remembered her face through the window as Papi steered her toward the sidewalk.

"She was nothing special. Why?"

"You might have to go to the shoe shop if I need to help Señora Rodriguez again."

"Oh... Can I stay outside then?"

"Only for a little bit. Carmen's been crazy ever since last week. She thinks if Miguel is out of her sight for more than a few minutes that the world will explode."

Miguel fidgeted and Mami didn't notice. She walked inside, the screen door rattling shut behind her. We stayed silent as we heard her rapid, one-after-the-other footsteps recede down the hall – city-goers' footsteps that, if you lay still enough, you could hear going late at night when she moved pots and pans around, cleaning up the kitchen. Papi trudged after her. He shut the screen door without a sound.

In my head I replayed everything that had happened. I thought about Tío Rodrigo in our living room, saying there was nothing to be done. I thought about Sister Tula smacking Maria Viramontes for being different like José Martí. I thought about Mami kissing me on the forehead that morning, saying I must tell no one of the lights at the dead house. I thought about Papi shifting at the mention of Celia's name. I thought about Pingüino's stupid letter home, and Luis yelling at the two strangers, and Señora Rodriguez crying in the hallways of her house with lemon juice dripping down her dress. I thought about Señor Moreno's anger and Señora Valle's grief and the helplessness of it all. And it made my stomach feel too full, like it was a bag filled to the brim with liquids and I was a water tower about to topple over because there were so many ugly things sifting around inside. I couldn't handle one more secret. I couldn't handle one more person telling me to be quiet. Not one more drop.

"Adela," Miguel said, "I have something to tell you."

I lay in bed that night recalling Miguel leaning against the blue wall of our house as a lizard scrambled above his head. I remembered the tree at the side of the house we'd stood next to so Mami wouldn't hear us, and the shadow one of the leaves had made, a straight dim diagonal across his face.

There was something wrong with Tío Rodrigo. Miguel wouldn't tell me what it was, but it had to be bad because there had been droplets of sweat forming at the crown of his head as he said it and Miguel never sweat, not even when he played baseball in the summer. Miguel didn't know what was wrong with Tío Rodrigo. He was just different. Off. He'd been coming home late recently. He had always come home late every once in a while, but so far it had been almost every night that week. On some nights he refused to eat dinner. When he did, he ate little – only small servings of rice and beans and never any meat. The oddest thing was this: he couldn't stand the sound of bones breaking.

Miguel loved snapping the bones of his chicken and sucking out the marrow. On the few occasions over the last couple of weeks when Tío Rodrigo made it home on time for dinner, Miguel would crack the bones of the wing to slurp out the insides. And every time, Tío Rodrigo would wince and claim he needed to go to the bathroom. But a few nights ago, twenty minutes after dinner had come and gone, Miguel passed by the bathroom to get a glass of water, and he saw Tío Rodrigo's shadow under the doorway. When he moved closer, he heard labored breathing. The panicky kind.

"There's something wrong with him," Miguel told me. "And I think there may be something wrong with me too."

"What do you mean?"

"Ever since last week, since – you know – the bombing, I can't walk on the street. I've done it a million times. I've walked from Marianao to the Hotel Nacional in Vedado a million times in the dark past kids and women and men and drunks and maybe I got nervous, but I was never scared. Now it's like every time I see people reach for their pockets or stop to talk to someone, I feel like running and I can't breathe. I know it's dumb because I've done it a million times before. It's just that… the way I breathe on my walk to work is what my dad sounded like on the other side of that door."

It had been another day of the shoe shop: warm gust of leather air, Dulce (this time, licking a cherry lollipop) with her feet up on the desk, the fan whining like its lungs were full of dust, the leather shoes sweating in the heat. And no Celia. A few customers strayed in and out, but none had her dark skin or her tiny waist or her clothes that were raggedy but pretty the way the feathers of dirty pigeons were, the ones in the alleyways of Old Havana that still had some gloss in them.

Every time the bell rang, Papi's eyes flicked towards the door and then back to whatever shoe he was shining at his desk, his fingers black even though he knew better than to get the powder on his hands. And Dulce daydreamed at the ceiling, her lips coloring into the red of the lollipop. When it was time to go, we piled into Abuelo's car and Papi took a plain white shoebox and put it under the seat next to him.

By the time we got home, there was an orangey sherbert in the sky and the sun glowed a hot-iron red with no halo. Me and Pingüino got out of the car and walked to the front door, leaving Papi behind in the front seat of Abuelo's car to smoke a cigarette. It wasn't uncommon for Abuelo or Mami or Papi to smoke a cigar on the front porch every once in a while, to see one of them blow smoke rings into the air, but cigarettes were different and I'd never seen Papi smoke one before. The smoke was something I wasn't used to. It was a white kind of acrid that lingered in the back of my throat long after I'd inhaled it.

When Pingüino and I opened the front door, Señora Valle and Mami were on the couch and they jumped in alarm. Scattered across the coffee table were papers with childlike handwriting. Señora Valle gathered them and pressed them to her chest. When she got up, she gazed at her doll shoes. I couldn't help noticing how small her feet were.

"I should go," Señora Valle said to the floor. "Thank you, Deianeira. God bless you."

"*Adiós.* Take care."

As Señora Valle swung open the screen door, Papi was on the other side, his hand about to grasp the handle. "Oh… *Buenos días*, Señora Valle."

"*Buenos días*, Señor Santiago."

Señora Valle scrambled out the door and down the stairs towards her house. Pingüino and I put our stuff down at the couch as Papi watched Señora Valle from behind the curtains. Mami was in the kitchen. She pulled out the big pan from the bottom drawer and a yellow-and-green tin can of olive oil from the pantry. I sat on one of the stools at the kitchen counter and Pingüino did too. Mami didn't reach for the radio. Papi made sure Señora Valle was out of sight before speaking, his voice tinged with iron.

"What was she doing here?"

Mami twisted the knob on the stove near the front, the one that hadn't gotten loose and popped off yet, the one that was rusting around the edges. "She wanted to speak with me."

"I thought it was Señora Rodriguez you were helping."

"I am helping her, but I'm helping Señora Valle too."

"With what?"

"I can't tell you."

"Why not?"

"Don't worry about it."

Papi stood over Mami. He was so close she must've felt his breath on her shoulder. She ignored him as she shifted the pots and pans around. Mami hefted the bag of yellow rice from the pantry and placed it on the counter.

"It better not be illegal," Papi said.

"Why would it be illegal?"

Papi ran his hands through his hair. "We've talked about this. We can't get any more involved with the Valles than normal."

"Sebastián, if you start with one of your *rebelde* theories –"

"It doesn't matter what I think about the Valles. It matters what *they* think. The police are watching us. They're always watching us. Even Rodrigo is probably watching us. There's a rat somewhere in this town, I can smell it. If someone sees you with her, then what will they think? What if they think we're involved? What if we're next? What if the next person kidnapped in the middle of the night is you or me or worse – What if it's Pingüino or Adela? There is no one we can trust. We're alone."

"Why are you so hopeless? Why do you erase the good in everything?"

"You can't erase the good if it was never there in the first place."

"What?"

"I mean – I don't... I didn't mean to say that. What I'm trying to say, Deianeira, is that I can't control the world around us. No one can. The best any of us can do is survive."

"And what about living? What about that?"

"Survival comes first."

"You're unbelievable. Just because you're insecure doesn't mean the rest of us have to be."

"I never said that."

"No, but you're trying to make it that way. Do you ever think about what you do?"

"What do you mean?"

"Nothing. Never mind. I don't know why I try anymore."

Pingüino's bottom lip quivered. It was easy to forget sometimes he was only ten. I was reminded of that as his child hands were splayed on the counter in front of him, his fingernails like dainty chiclets glowing in the dark.

"The meetings at this house are over," Papi said. "I forbid you to bring either Señora Valle or Señora Rodriguez here ever again. Is that clear?" Mami glared at him, and went back to the stove.

Papi grabbed her by the shoulders and wrenched her towards him.

"Get your hands off me!" she screamed.

"Is that clear?" he said again.

Mami tried ripping herself from him, and they struggled a moment before he released her.

"*Imbécil*," she said, and I could taste the poison soaked into the words, could feel a sour aftertaste as the rest of them came out of her mouth. "I should have never married you."

And what hurt the most wasn't the poison or the anger or the hot-iron sun in the sky searing into oblivion. It wasn't Pingüino's child hands or Señora Valle's cramped doll shoes or Papi's cigarette smoke searing itself into the back of my throat. It was the tiredness creased into Papi's face, the sad wrinkles that sagged around the deadness in his eyes, the slow acceptance and indifference with which he absorbed Mami's words one by one and said absolutely nothing at all.

The night they met the whole city stopped glowing. That's how Papi always started it.

From afar, the city was a shell in the moonlight. Shining, white, ghostly. The buildings rising up. Ethereal. But on the streets it was different. The pavement hummed. Salsa pounded the concrete, prostitutes lounged with their legs gleaming, cigar smoke drifted along the alleyways. And there was rum – a whole lot of it.

The boy was a mess. He was one of those country boys who'd never been to the city, the one who'd learned salsa from his grandmother in the parlor while his aunts stood around and made fun. The first time he rode in a car, he was twenty and it was the taxi from the train station to the University. He had a wisp for a mustache and doe eyes.

The girl was a queen with dark hair and even darker eyes. The first time he saw her smile, all there was was bright lipstick and the teensiest gap between her two front teeth. It was easy to imagine: a mint on her breath, red nail polish that smelled like alcohol, hips that swayed to the beat of a Latin rhythm. The golden studs her mother gave her. Her neck sticky with sweat because she was the first one on the dance floor and the last to leave. He saw her and the streets stopped humming.

It used to be Papi would gather me and Pingüino on the couch in the living room, and tell the story in his loudest voice so Mami could hear it all the way in the kitchen, or the bedroom, or the hallway, or wherever she was in the house. Abuelo would sit in his big green armchair while Pingüino groaned and put a pillow over his head. And Mami would appear at the doorway with her arms crossed.

"*Y aquí está la muchacha hermosa* – Here is the beautiful girl!"

Inevitably, Mami – the girl who had grown up and become even *more* beautiful, Papi said – would let out a giggle, and she would let Papi sweep her into his arms. He would have trouble picking her up because of the bottom of whatever dress she was wearing, would complain of the pain in his back (*"Pero Dios mío*, the boy has gotten old, hasn't he?"), and Abuelo, Pingüino, and I would laugh at their ridiculousness, at the mango-red blush creeping its way across Mami's face. They would kiss and all would be right with the world.

Papi hadn't told the story in ages.

The morning after Señora Valle and the papers, Papi was out on the porch smoking another cigarette. I woke up early and saw his outline pixelated by the mesh of the screen door. There was a mess of blankets and cushions on the floor of the living room. Papi had spent another night on the couch. He was wrapped in the thin blanket that smelled of mothballs. Next to him, a foggy glass was half-filled with rum that hadn't seen daylight since *Nochebuena* last year.

I opened the door and stood barefoot on the porch, the floor cool with early morning.

"Can I sit with you?"

A slow sad nod. The sound of a lizard scrabbling against the wood.

I sat next to him, unwrapped part of the cover, and leaned into his chest. He smelled of rum and sleeplessness. He put a weak arm around me.

"*Ay mi* Adelita. What are we going to do?"

I said nothing, and felt a faint fear that maybe I would have to. My stomach felt as if I was about to cry. Papi sighed and studied my hair.

"Your hair glows in the sunlight, did you know?"

I grabbed a strand and held it up to my eyes. "It looks dark to me."

"No, *mija*, not like that," Papi said, chuckling weakly. "It's along the edges. It turns golden in the sun."

"I guess."

The sun moved across the sky a few more inches before I dared to speak.

"Do you still love her?"

Papi was silent for a good few moments before responding. I tried to see if I could find any of that boy in him, that ruggedness, that sweetness that Mami fell for. I tried so hard, and refused to admit I had found nothing. I remembered the way he had grabbed her, and his arm around me felt heavy and dull. Papi took a sip from the foggy glass.

"Of course I do."

I got that crying feeling in my stomach again, and ignored the heaviness inside me. I took hold of Papi's hand, and felt the country boy calloused fingers that weren't glowing anymore, but were colored the gray of cigarette ash drifting lost in still air.

"Tell me the story again, Papi."

He went quiet. So quiet, I could hear the wind moving between the leaves. Then, he began, in a voice as bittersweet as an old Cuban folk song.

"The night they met the whole city stopped glowing..."

As I listened, I watched the shadows move across the green of the lawn, the blue of the raggedy old house of Marianao where Mami and Papi had begun together, the front porch steps that had long since splintered in the heat. It felt like hours, but me and Papi, we were awake watching the world move together, huddled beneath the sunrise and a thin, mothball blanket.

Every day at around noon, Mami put on her dress that smelled of oldness, slipped on a pair of worn brown sandals, and checked the mail at the rotten clump of mailboxes in the overgrown jungle by the intersection. We didn't get much in the mail other than the odd letter from Tía Noelia, Papi's sister who lived on the plantation, and the money that Papi's uncle sent every few weeks. But on Friday, there was an extra bit of mail no one had been expecting, certainly not Pingüino. That day, me and Pingüino walked home from school, and as soon as we walked through the front door –

"What do you mean you put lizards in the teacher's desk?"

Pingüino froze. "What?"

From his armchair, Abuelo chuckled, and put down that day's newspaper to watch. "You're in for it now, *mijo*."

"What?"

"Letter from your school today." Mami threw an envelope on the coffee table. The top of it had already been ripped open. "Read it."

Pingüino picked it up, and I read over his shoulder:

*Dear Señora Santiago,*

*We write to inform you of conduct on the part of your son, Pedro Santiago, unbefitting of la Escuela Católica de la Virgen María. The conduct in question consisted of placing lizards in the desk of his teacher, Sister Juana, severely scaring her and causing one student to faint...* (I skimmed on) ... *This is Pedro's third offense, and in accordance with school policy we send this letter both with Pedro himself and in the mail. We hope this finds you well and that you will discuss the matter with Pedro in order to stop any further instances of incorrigible behavior.*

*Cordialmente,*

*Sister Moye*
*Directora de la Escuela Católica de la Virgen María*

"Do you have anything to say for yourself?" Mami said.

"No. Except Sister Juana is a real screamer."

A ridiculous half-stifled laugh came out of me and Abuelo at the same time. Abuelo covered his mouth with his hand, and then slowly lifted his newspaper to cover his face. His forehead was bright pink beneath his hairline. Mami had that I'm-going-to-smack-you look on her face.

"The next time you talk back like that, *te voy a dar una galleta.* I'm going to hit you so hard you won't even know what year it is."

Pingüino swallowed a grin. "*Sí, Mami.*"

"What did you do with the letter?"

The grin disappeared. "What letter?"

"The letter she sent home with you."

"I may have lost it."

"Don't talk shit *porque me tienes hasta el último pelo.* What did you do with it?"

"I threw it away."

Mami's nostrils flared. "You are grounded for three weeks starting today. No television, no baseball, no dessert, no going out during the weekends. And you're going to help me put the laundry up."

"*Pero Mami,* that's a sissy job."

"No, it's not. Now go to your room."

Pingüino retreated and I dumped my bags on the couch. I sat on the arm of Abuelo's chair. Meanwhile, Abuelo sighed and laid the newspaper flat on his lap. "*Ya no puedo con las noticias.* I can't take the newspapers anymore."

"I don't know why you're surprised," Mami said. She was at the sink, cleaning a plate with an old blue rag.

"You haven't even read it," I said.

"I don't have to. What is it? Someone got shot. Someone was arrested. Some rebels in the mountains. Batista says everything is fine. A lot of people were shot. A lot of people were arrested. The rebels are winning. The rebels aren't winning. Batista still says everything is fine. Everybody died. Is it ever anything different?"

"No," Abuelo said, "but they're still people."

Mami continued scrubbing as if she hadn't heard. Even from the living room, I could see the plate she was cleaning was already spotless, could hear the grating of the fibers on ceramic, could see the pink rawness of her fingertips.

"Well, no one remembers that anymore."

Abuelo sighed. He folded the newspaper, and placed it on the floor by his feet. "Where's Sebastián?"

"At work. Where else?"

Abuelo glanced at me. "I heard the arguing the other day."

Mami stopped scrubbing. "You did?"

"I hear most things. I may be old, but I'm not deaf. Is everything –?"

"Everything is as it always is." Mami put the rag and the plate aside, "I think I'm going to take a nap. I have a headache."

She left the room and I listened as her footsteps faded down the hall. I heard the door close behind her. Abuelo patted my hand. "Adela," he said, "Do me a favor and turn on the television for me. Let's see if there's anything worth watching, eh?"

It was Saturday and it was about to rain. The sky was white the way it was before a thunderstorm. It was fine because Pingüino was grounded and I didn't feel like walking over to Miguel's house anyway. At one point, Mami told us she was going to the grocery store, but other than that, the day had been uneventful. Now we were in our room staring at the ceiling.

"Adela?" Pingüino said, splayed out on his bed.

"What?" I said, splayed out on mine.

"I'm hungry."

"Then go get something to eat."

Pingüino rolled over onto his face. "No," he said into the pillow.

"Then why are you complaining?"

He rolled back over into a more regular position. "Because I'm hungry."

"I'm not going to get you something to eat."

"Why not?"

"You have legs, don't you?"

"You'd let your little brother starve?"

"In a heartbeat."

"You're horrible."

A long pause.

"Adela?"

"What?"

"Do you think Mami and Papi are going to break up?"

I wasn't sure how to respond. I thought about what Padre Francisco had said about telling the truth, so I decided to try as much as I could. "I don't know," I confessed.

He sighed, and seemed sad.

"Goddamn it," I said, getting up.

"What?"

"What do you want to eat?"

"*Ropa vieja*," Pingüino said.

"Try again, *comemierda*."

"Fine. Ham-and-cheese sandwich."

"Better."

I walked into the living room and Papi was pacing. There was a woman on the couch and I realized with a start that the woman wasn't Mami. It was Celia. She wore lipstick and a skimpy red dress. "Oh, it's Adela," Celia said in a mild voice. "*Hola* Adela."

Papi stopped pacing. He closed his eyes. "*Mierda*," he whispered. He rubbed his face. "Adela. I thought you were in your room with Pingüino. Abuelo's still asleep, isn't he?"

I was so appalled I had trouble speaking. "What – What is she doing here?"

"Go back to your room."

"You can't tell her what to do," Celia said.

"Sure, I can. She's my daughter."

"She's a person," she said to Papi. "You're a person," she told me as if I didn't already know, "You do what you want to do."

I regarded her skimpy red dress. "She's a whore, isn't she?" I asked Papi.

"You don't have to be so rude about it," Celia said, checking her nails.

"What?" Papi said.

"She's a whore. Just like the girl you screamed at."

"What girl?" Papi said.

"You don't remember? You were laughing with Pingüino about something and there was a prostitute standing at the curb and you called her a *puta* through the window."

"What does that have to do with anything?"

"Everything!" Celia said, standing up. "It's a lack of *love* is what it is."

"Shhh," Papi said, "Do you want the whole house to hear?"

"Is she crazy or something?" I said.

"Why can't you tell me?" Celia said.

"Why do you need to know?" Papi said.

"Because it's not enough."

Papi glanced at me. "Not here."

"For God's sake, Sebastián. Your kids saw me at the shoe shop and now I'm in your house. I know that Adela, for one, isn't stupid."

"Mami's going to be home soon," I said.

"See? She's already figured it out. Go on, Adela. Tell your father what you know."

"What?"

"You're a smart girl. You already know what I am, tell him what else you know."

I hesitated before saying it. "You're having an affair."

Celia smiled, "There you go."

Papi threw his hands in the air. "Has the whole world gone mad?"

"Yes. Isn't it wonderful?"

"What is wrong with you?"

"I love you. I've never been in love before."

"Stop saying that."

"Why can't you tell me you love me too?"

"I'm married."

"That hasn't stopped you before."

"I never said I loved you."

"I just want to know, Sebastián, please?"

Papi sighed and sat on the couch, rubbing his temples.

"You know, Mami is going to be home soon and – Where are you going?"

Papi got up and walked outside. I gazed at Celia and she shrugged. I went to the window and watched as he ripped open the door of Abuelo's car to rummage around beneath the seats. He came out of the car with a white box in his hands. It was the box from the shoe shop. The sky became a dark, violent gray, and the rain poured. The raindrops struck the hood of Abuelo's car so hard it sounded as if it were being bludgeoned with marbles. The road in front of our house turned into a rippling river, the rain making the surface dance. Papi stood with the white box in the downpour, his clothes soaked, his bare feet in the mud. His hair was plastered. Through the window our eyes met.

"Wait, what's she doing here?" Pingüino walked out from the hall and he eyed Celia as she stood in the corner.

"It's complicated, *mijo*," she said, and lit a cigarette. It filled the air with a white acrid scent.

"You can't smoke in here," Pingüino said.

"Why not?"

"I don't know," he said. "You just can't."

"Those are the same cigarettes Papi was smoking the other day," I said.

"Hmmm," Celia said. She took a drag and blew out the smoke. "Wonder who got him hooked."

Papi came back in and shoved the soaking white box into Celia's hands. "Here you go. If that doesn't tell you what you need to know, I don't know what will."

She took off the top, and there was a crackling of tissue paper. "Oh," she said. "They're beautiful." She picked up one of the red shoes from the inside and I recognized them as the tattered flamenco shoes she'd fallen in love with on that day in the shoe shop.

"I was going to clean them and make them new, but you didn't give me the chance."

"Who *is* she?" Pingüino said.

"Papi's girlfriend."

Pingüino blinked, "What?"

The front door crashed open. Mami stood in the doorway with two giant wet paper bags full of groceries. They were slipping out of her hands. "Adela," she said, "Help me please, they're falling."

I rushed forward to grab the bags by the bottom, but it was too late. The cans of olive oil, the tomatoes, the bag of rice, the milk carton, the red peppers, the chicken, the onions, the garlic, the black beans, the bread, the cheese, the eggs – all of it came tumbling out onto the floor. The eggs cracked and the milk spilled. The tomatoes rolled across the floor.

"*¡COÑO!*" Mami screamed.

"*¿Qué carajo está pasando?*" Abuelo said, emerging from his room. "Can't a man sleep in peace?"

Mami noticed Celia for the first time. "Who are you?"

"Papi's girlfriend," Pingüino said, "Apparently."

I wanted to strangle him, but mostly I wanted to strangle Papi.

"She's his what?" Abuelo said.

"Celia, get out of here," Papi said.

"But I –"

"NOW!"

Mami picked up one of the cans of olive oil off the floor and threw it at Papi. "I KNEW IT! YOU BASTARD!"

"Celia, get out of here!"

Celia did as she was told. She shoved her red shoes back into the box and disappeared into the rain.

"*¿ESA PUTA?* THAT WHORE? THAT'S WHO YOU'RE SLEEPING WITH?"

"Deianeira, *por favor, cálmate.* Please calm down –"

## "HOW *DARE* YOU TELL ME TO CALM DOWN?"

She picked up another can of olive oil and chucked it at his head. He ducked just in time. She stormed over and kicked him, slapped him, raked him with her nails. And he didn't even fight back. He curled into himself and took it. She scratched his cheek and it began to bleed. It took a few seconds for Abuelo to intervene and pull her off of him. She crumpled to the floor, sobbing. But it was all over her – the blood. Papi's blood. I never thought a cut on the cheek would bleed so much. The scent of it mingled with the acridness of Celia's cigarette smoke. Abuelo got on the floor and rocked her like she was a little kid saying "Shhh, shhh."

Papi wiped the blood on his pants even though he was wet. His fingers were covered in red, running into the lines of his handprints. He saw us, standing by the couch. It was then that I realized I had wrapped my arms around Pingüino, that I was holding his head against my chest so he wouldn't have to see. He had begun to cry and his mucus and saliva soaked into my shirt.

"Go to your room," Papi said.

"Come on," I whispered to Pingüino. "Come on, let's go."

He wouldn't move. Mami yowled while Abuelo wiped her face with his shirtfront and murmured things to her. Papi went into the kitchen and cleaned his cheek with one of the towels Mami kept by the oven.

"*Vámonos*," I said to Pingüino. I unwrapped myself from him, and guided him towards the room, his nose running. There was a loose blanket on the floor – the same thin, dusty one me and Papi had wrapped around ourselves as we sat beneath the sunrise – and Pingüino stumbled over its mangled form like it was road kill. In our room, he collapsed onto his bed facedown, paralyzed, with a muffled scream of "*¿Por qué, por qué, por qué?*" And because I could not answer, I sat next to him and stroked his feathery hair that resembled Papi's as I told myself I would not cry though my insides felt dead. He sobbed as if the world were ending, and perhaps it was. In the room next door, voices murmured. When I went to the window, the neighborhood lights were on.

Papi met Celia by accident in December before Christmastime. It was Jorge Luciano's bachelor party, and Papi said he couldn't say no, that Jorge had been one of his only friends from college who'd come from the same dirt he had way out in the countryside, that they'd grown up a few miles away from each other, which in those parts was like living right next door. He'd told him he didn't want to go to a brothel, but Jorge wouldn't listen and so he'd been dragged along in a car full of *borrachos*, drunk on cheap rum with stains all down their fronts. Celia was the prostitute they'd given him, and he swore he hadn't slept with her that first time. It was just talking about dumb things like his job at the shoe shop and his kids and the rebellion and how damn bored he'd been lately going in an endless cycle from home to work and back again, about his family in Marianao and how useless he felt in the Zapatería de Cuba in Old Havana where the same customers filed in and out and Dulce sat bored at her desk... That's how they had found out the funny coincidence; Celia was Dulce's sister. So they got to talking in the alleyway outside the brothel, smoking cigarettes while Jorge Luciano and the boys disappeared to God-knows-where. The whole city was dressed up for Christmas, the signs all down the street looped up in golden garland, yellow stars, copper bells – even the furniture stores and the barber shops were decked out.

That was how it began. Everything after that was just details. Celia would loiter outside the shoe shop on certain afternoons, bright ones when the toothless man on the corner sold bags of oranges to stopped cars on the intersections, gloomy ones when the flags outside people's shops fluttered harshly in the wind. It became so that those days Celia showed up outside the doorstep were sacred days, like finding a peso lodged in the cracks of the cobblestone. She was a radiant indulgence, one Papi had no plans of falling in love with.

The first and last time Papi slept with Celia was on a Wednesday – March 20, 1957. The same day as the bombing at the Hotel Nacional. It was at her place, a tiny box-shaped apartment in the ghettoes where the buildings were tangled in laundry lines heavy with clothing. The place itself was only a few years old, but the poverty of its residents had worn it down until it was as pathetic as Celia's saggy old mattress. He told Mami that after they were finished, as he dressed himself to leave, he looked out the window, saw the glowing white façade of Havana in the distance, and broke down as he was reminded of Mami and how in love he'd been the night he first saw her. He resolved he would never see Celia again, no matter how radiant her smile was, no matter how much he felt he needed a break from the monotony of home and work and Marianao and the rusted bell that barely ever rang in the Zapatería. He told Celia too, that very night. But she hadn't believed him. *You'll come back for me*, she'd told him in the squalor of her apartment. *You always do.*

Except she'd come for him over and over again. The whole thing was a mistake, Papi knew that now. He should have never done it.

"So you never loved her?" Mami asked, at the end.

It was night now and the rain had died down to a cloud of dampness hanging over the street. Pingüino had fallen asleep in his bed, in the same position he had first collapsed, the tears dried onto his cheeks. Mami and Papi were in the living room with a single lamp on. I was curled up in the hallway, listening. I'd been there so long I felt my bones were going to meld into the wall, that I would be fossilized there forever. Papi's voice was parched for forgiveness.

"No," he said.

"Why are you here?"

"Because I love you. I know that now."

"You weren't sure?"

"Deianeira, please…"

"I gave up everything when I married you."

"I know."

"I gave you thirteen years of my life when I could have been anything."

"I know – I know that. I'm sorry."

"Sorry? Is that all you have?"

"Are you going to kick me out?"

"I don't know. Tell me the truth this time."

"About what?"

"Do you love her?"

"It's not like that."

"What's it like then?"

"I don't know. But it's not as straightforward as either of us would like it to be."

"Then why did you do it?"

"I told you. I felt – trapped."

"By what?"

"Everything."

"That's not an answer."

"Do you remember what I said about survival?"

"That it comes before living?"

"Yes."

"What about it?"

"It was survival."

"Why do you get to survive and I don't?"

"What?"

"You don't know anything, do you?"

"I guess not. Are you going to kick me out?"

"No. Not tonight."

A dim light flooded the hall. I thought Abuelo had retreated to his room, but now he stood over me without his glasses.

"*Vámonos, mi* Adelita," he told me. He talked in barely a whisper. He took my hand and helped me up. "I think it's time to go to bed."

He did the same thing Papi used to do when we were little. He carried me to my room, put me in my bed, and pulled the covers up to my chest. Then he kissed me on the forehead, and said "*Buenas noches*, Delita." When he closed the door, I watched until the light beneath my door faded away. As soon as it was gone, I fell into a troubled sleep.

The house was quiet. Pingüino was asleep in his bed, Papi was passed out on the couch with a blanket, and nothing stirred behind Abuelo's closed door. If a stranger had seen our living room that morning, they would have found nothing amiss; the twirling dust mites of the air, the couches so still it was as if they wanted to talk, the kitchen spotless, all the occupants of a perfect blue house dozing peacefully. But there were small things. Bits of eggshell on the floor. Dents in the wall from the cans of olive oil. Papi's shapeless form beneath the covers. Half-wet streaks of blood and rainwater. Most of the evidence had been swept away, but not all of it. I went to Mami's room and found the door half-cracked. I pushed it open.

Inside there was nothing but a pile of empty sheets. She was gone. Her black church heels were missing from the closet and so was one of her nice dresses, a lilac one she'd bought a few years ago from somebody's sister. I told myself she'd probably gone to church for some alone time and that was it, but I wasn't so sure. It was unlike her. Then again, most of what had been going on was unlike her. Mami had never cried before. Not once. Not even a few years ago when a friend from college, Cele, was killed accidentally when she walked into a shootout between the police and a couple of kids trying to rob a jewelry store. In the end nothing was stolen, the windows of the jewelry store were obliterated, the policemen were unharmed, one of the robbers suffered from a broken pinky, and Cele was facedown in a puddle of blood at the center of the street, a shopping bag in her hand containing a new satin bullet-bra and some underwear. When Mami heard, she was wordless for a few days. Later, she left to visit Cele's parents in Cerro and after she came back, it was as if nothing had happened. Everything was normal again. I didn't know how things would go from here on out.

I was light-footed when I went to the kitchen. I tried not to wake Papi whose snoring drifted through the air. In the sink, I saw two dirty cups and a pair of spoons with speckles along the edges. They were from Señora Rodriguez's house, from that strange day with the lemonade and Luis and Señora Rodriguez sobbing in the hallway.

Without thinking, I grabbed the cups and spoons, slipped on some sandals from my room, and stumbled out of the house in my nightgown. I walked the two houses down to Señora Rodriguez's house and banged on the door. I didn't expect anyone to be there, but I felt like pounding on somebody's door. It was Sunday morning and most of Marianao was deserted, the people packed into sweaty pews at church with the doors open. Which was why I almost fell over when Señora Rodriguez's door swung open, and behind it was Luis, a fresh bruise blooming across his cheek. The middle of it was eggplant-purple. I couldn't see much else of his face since it was in shadow.

"Oh… *Hola* Luis. I don't know if you remember me, but my name's Adela. I was here last week with my brother, Pingüino. Your mother made lemonade, and she told us to bring over the cups and spoons when we were done."

"*Hola* Adela," Luis said, smiling. "Of course, I remember you."

I waited for him to go pale and fall over or something, but he just stood there smiling, which must have hurt with the bruise on his cheek. I cleared my throat, "I forgot to wash the glasses over at my house. Do you mind if I wash them in your sink?"

"Sure you can. I'm not doing anything important anyway."

It was only after I was across the threshold that I realized a series of unfortunate facts: (1) I was alone with Luis Rodriguez in an empty house; (2) I was dressed only in my nightgown and sandals; (3) no one knew where I was; (4) there was probably a reason why Señora Rodriguez had chosen to leave Luis at home rather than take him to church; and (5) almost every home within the immediate vicinity was deserted with the exception of my house whose occupants were asleep. On the other hand, Luis was acting like a normal person today. Besides, it was too late to change my mind. I was already in.

As I moved into Señora Rodriguez's kitchen, the familiar sights greeted me. The blue-and-white wallpaper peeling near the ceiling, and the sink lined with rust, and the big windows in the back with the lemon tree brambles peering over the bottom edge. I put the cups and the spoons on the counter. Luis installed himself in a seat in the corner. Now that his face was in the light, I could see a nasty gash on his forehead that had already scabbed over.

"How's school?" Luis asked.

"Fine."

"What are you learning about?"

"José Martí."

"Oh, good. I love José Martí."

"I don't know why people like him so much."

"He's the classic hero, I guess."

"Not really. He got shot. That's not very heroic."

"You're right," Luis said, laughing. "That's not heroic at all."

I was shocked because I'd never heard him laugh before, and he had a nice laugh. It was airy and carefree. "You agree with me?" I said.

"Yes, I suppose I do," he said, amused. "But I think it's better that way. It makes him different."

"But why do you love him so much?"

"He was a very hopeful man. Have you ever heard of –?"

"*Cultivo una rosa blanca?*" I said, finishing his sentence.

"Yes. Are they teaching that in school now?"

"No. It's my father's favorite poem."

"Must be a good man then."

I stayed silent.

"Did he tell you the origin story?"

"No."

"Rumor has it José Martí wrote the poem in jail after a friend turned him in to Spanish authorities."

"Not a very good friend then."

"No, he wasn't. But Martí forgave him anyway. If you choose to see it that way."

"What other way is there to see it?"

Luis shrugged. "It's poetry. Count the number of people on the planet and then multiply it by infinity. That's how many meanings a poem can have."

"He couldn't have just forgiven him like that, could he?"

"I suppose it could have been a form of defiance. He did send it to him afterwards."

"Well, if my friend did something like that to me, I'd probably want to kill him."

"I think that may have been the point."

"To kill him?"

"No," Luis said. I waited for him to explain, but he didn't.

I went over to the sink and began washing the cups and spoons with a pink rag I found at the bottom along with a few bloated grains of rice. When I reached for the soap, I saw there was a towel with some blood on it, though not as much as the one Papi had used last night. I figured it was for the gash on Luis's forehead, and I pretended not to see it as the water from the faucet came out with violent force, splattering against the metal bottom of the sink.

"What happened to your face?" I said.

"I fell."

"Oh," I said, not believing him. "My dad fell too, just yesterday. He cut open his cheek and there was so much blood, like you wouldn't believe. It got all over the floor, and I think my mother forgot to clean it up, so it's still there. It's eerie walking by a puddle of blood, even when you know the reason it's there isn't that big of a deal…"

I was finished with the first cup and I moved on to the second, my sleeves turning transparent from the water.

"You know, my brother would have been here, but he got punished. He put lizards in the teacher's desk and then ripped up the letter the principal sent home."

"Your brother couldn't come?"

I was finished with the second cup, and now I was on to the spoons, scrubbing over the rough spots of rust on the handles. "No."

"Does he know you're here?"

I felt self-conscious in my nightgown all of a sudden. I had the uncomfortable feeling that Luis's eyes were boring into my back where my bra would be if I had to wear one, that he was trying to stare straight through my nightgown. A wisp of hair fell in front of my face and I blew it away because my hands were wet. I considered lying, but something told me if I lied, Luis would see right through me.

"No."

I jumped as Luis's chair rasped against the floor. The ceiling was high so the sound echoed and grated. An army of goosebumps sprouted on my arms. Luis was leaning across the countertop, his hair stringy and greasy and drooping over, his bruise brighter in the light.

"Can I tell you something?"

I was very aware of the spoon still in my hand, the soap suds still slippery on my fingers.

"I lied," he said, and his voice went soft. "I didn't fall. It was those two men you saw at church."

I wanted to put down the spoon, and turn off the water that was pummeling the sink and whining through the faucet. But if I moved, something in the air would break. He would stop, and I would never know about the two strangers.

"Who are they?"

"Who are they?" Luis laughed, and this time it didn't sound nice at all. "It doesn't matter who they are. But you understand, Adela, don't you? You know about lying too. We're liars, the both of us."

"I don't know what you're talking about."

"Your father did not fall."

Something got caught in my throat. "What?"

"Your father," Luis said, emphasizing each word, "did not fall. I saw it, Adela. A woman in a skimpy red dress goes in. Your mother goes in after her. The skimpy woman leaves. The screaming travels through the night. It's not hard to figure out what happens next."

"Why are you telling me this?"

"Do you love your father?"

"What?"

"Do you love your father?"

I stared at him.

"It's a hell of a hard road to forgiveness."

I rinsed my hands beneath the running water. My eyes were tearing up, but I didn't want Luis to see. So I turned off the water with some effort (even the handle was rusted), and gazed at the corner where the wall met the ceiling, where the wallpaper was peeling and revealed an ugly brown stain.

"Please forgive me," Luis said. He sounded as if he was about to cry.

I wondered if I should walk over and comfort him, but I shuddered at the thought of putting my hand on his shoulder. Instead, I left the cups and the spoons in the sink with the bloated grains of rice, and I walked around the countertop and sat at the stool next to him, the same stool I had sat in the week before as Señora Rodriguez had squeezed lemons into the juicer.

"Forgive you for what?"

Luis took off his glasses and cleaned them on his shirt. Without them, his head was like a gigantic cantaloupe with pushpins for eyes, and when he put them back on, his glasses were even foggier than before.

"Do you like President Batista, Adela?"

"I – I don't –"

Luis leapt from his chair and grabbed my shoulders, "Don't you see? How everyone is too scared to say it? And if they don't say it, nothing gets done. I *did* something, Adela."

"What did you do?"

He let me go and I gripped the counter, my heartbeat shuddering in my ears. And as I sat at the counter, I think he saw me clearly for the first time, saw the fear that must have been scrawled across my face, heard the words coming out of his mouth, and realized what they must have sounded like.

"I did the right thing," he said, "I swear."

I didn't care about being polite anymore. I didn't care that Luis was a sad, pitiful twenty-year-old who could go from discussing José Martí one moment to throttling thirteen-year-old girls the next. I didn't care about Señora Rodriguez or her cups and spoons I had abandoned in the sink next to the bloated rice grains and Luis's bloodied towel. I wanted to get out of that house, and I never wanted to set foot in it ever again.

And so, I left Luis sobbing against the countertop with his greasy drooping hair, and his tearstained glasses, and his eggplant-purple bruise. I walked out of the door past Señora Rodriguez's pristine white rocking chair and her coral-colored walls. And when I saw Señora Rodriguez on the street in Marianao on the way back from church with her hair rolled up and her soul-filled eyes, she waved, her purse draped over her arm. But I didn't wave back. Instead, I sprinted up the concrete stairs of my small blue house

and slammed the screen door behind me, never once thinking of
going back.

The two strangers were arrested a week and a half later. It was a hot afternoon on a weekday and Pingüino and Mami were pinning up damp laundry on the lines in the front yard which hung from the metal posts where the hammock used to be (Miguel and Pingüino broke it a few years ago when they both tried to get into it at the same time and the strings snapped). It had been a week and a half of Sister Tula teaching algebra and a chalkboard filled with Xs and Ys, of Miguel and I riding our bikes around Marianao feeding stray dogs while Pingüino stayed home and sulked, of Abuelo shaking his head every time he saw the news in *The Havana Post*, of Papi exiled to the couch at night ("My neck hurts *con cojones*," he said every time he rose with rat-nested hair in the mornings), of Mami slamming doors whenever Papi tried talking to her or woke up early to make Mami's favorite breakfast: *empanadas de queso*.

Pingüino had to do the job I normally did, and I watched, gloating, from the bottom step.

"How's it going, *hermanito*?" I said.

"Shut up," he told me.

"*Oye*," Mami said, "*Cállense los dos*."

Pingüino glared as he held the bowl of clothespins – a mixture of wooden, metal, and plastic ones, all of them a collection from years of Mami thinking she'd lost some, buying more, and then finding them again. Mami stood on a wobbly chair with one leg shorter than the others. She had to stretch a little bit to pin the wet dresses, the pants, the shirts, the bras, the underwear. At the moment it happened, Mami was pinning up my stuffed bunny with the pink ribbon on it Tía Carmen had given me as a baby. She'd washed it because as she went around picking up discarded clothing from the floor of our room, she saw Rubia (that was its name) and realized it was three shades darker than it was supposed to be from years of me drooling on it as I slept.

She had just clipped it up by the second ear, when we heard a scream from down the street in the direction of Señora Rodriguez's house. Mami almost fell from her chair, but she steadied herself by grabbing Pingüino's shoulder and digging her nails in.

"*¡Ay!*" He dropped the bowl on the floor, and the clothespins went everywhere.

"Sorry, Pingüino," Mami said, letting go. She stepped down, steadying herself on one of the posts. She peered down the street. "*¿Pero, coño, qué pasa?* What's happening?"

The answer came soon after. The two strangers were different than they had been a few weeks ago. Now, they were clean-shaven. They had gotten new shirts that were white and crisp like the just-washed linen I imagined was put on the beds of the Hotel Nacional every morning. They were running and there were sweat stains on their shirts. As they came closer, I saw that their eyes were red-rimmed and bulging.

Behind them was Tío Rodrigo. The last time I had seen him was two weeks ago at church when he watched Luis and the strangers on the lawn. In that time, he had become a stickman skinnier than even Miguel. The outline of his ribs was creased into his shirt, his shoulders had lost their broadness, and he seemed shrunken in his police uniform. His head was skeleton-like beneath his policeman's cap, the brown of his skin drawn taut over the hollows of his eyes and cheeks. A few feet behind him was Tío Rodrigo's partner, Manuel, a heavyset man with a thin mustache tickling his upper lip.

Tío Rodrigo was gaining on them. All around us, faces appeared at windows, and doors whined open. Señor Moreno came out onto his porch and squinted at the approaching figures. Señora Rodriguez did the same, clutching at the white rocking chair with one hand and at her heart with the other. Across from Señora Rodriguez's house, Señora Valle's face appeared at the window, Diego peeking around the curtain next to her.

Tío Rodrigo caught one of them right before they got to Rafi Consuelo's house. He tackled him and they both went sprawling onto the asphalt. Tío Rodrigo climbed on the man's back with the handcuffs and the man let out a guttural scream. Mami gasped. Pingüino flinched. Señora Valle swept the curtain across the windows. Señora Rodriguez put her hands over her mouth. Señor Moreno stumbled back inside.

"Manuel! *¡Agárralo!* He's getting away!" Tío Rodrigo said.

Manuel wheezed as he tackled the second man on Rafi Consuelo's uncut lawn. He cuffed him and the man spat blood and blades of grass from his mouth. Over on the asphalt, Tío Rodrigo was having issues restraining the first man. Mami stepped onto the sidewalk as if to help.

"Deianeira, stay over there... Where is the goddamn car?"

A black-and-white police car came squealing down the street and burnt rubber tore the air apart. The one with the grass in his mouth went quietly as Manuel shoved him in headfirst. His lips were smeared in blood and I could tell he thought he was about to die. Once in, he observed his lap as if he hadn't noticed it before.

The second man fought like hell. I recognized him as the one who had grabbed me at church, and now that he was in front of our house I could see that his knuckles were bruised from punching Luis in the face. The man bit Tío Rodrigo in the arm, and Tío Rodrigo pulled out his police baton. He pushed the man onto the hood of the car. He brought the baton down on the man's arm. A sickening crack, and a scream red with pain. The man's wrist broke, and it flopped onto the hood of the car. I had the sudden desire to vomit.

Tío Rodrigo straightened his policeman's cap, embarrassed, as if he'd been caught with his zipper down rather than breaking another man's wrist. After saying something to Manuel, he got into the car and drove away without a siren or a single flashing light.

My stuffed bunny had been the last item to be clipped up. I watched it hang from the line by its ears, swinging in the air with dark button-eyes as Mami, Pingüino, and I began to pick up the clothespins from the porch and the grass. Over on Señora Rodriguez's porch, the rocking chair still rocked, its emptiness wanting someone to touch it lightly, to make it all end.

Night had fallen and me and Pingüino were spread out in front of the television on our bellies, the carpet leaving imprints on our elbows. We were playing dominoes. Abuelo sat in his green chair watching television, and Mami was in the chair across from him flipping pages of an old book with great care. Papi was cooped up in his room listening to the radio as he had been for the past few days because no one wanted to talk to him.

"I've only got one left, Adela," Pingüino said. "Are you sure you don't want to give up?"

"I could still lock the game."

"And Miguel could get a girlfriend."

"You're mean."

"No, I'm not. I'm truthful."

I studied my dominoes, knowing I couldn't win. Abuelo tore his eyes away from the television, and leaned over my shoulder, studying my pieces with his tongue out.

"She can't lock me out, can she?" Pingüino asked.

Abuelo's face remained blank. "I have no idea."

"Whatever he says, don't listen to him," Mami said from her chair. "He's a horrible cheater."

"I am not," Abuelo said. He leaned closer and whispered, "She's just upset because I always win."

Mami rolled her eyes, half-smiling. She closed the book and laid it on her lap.

"Mami, what are you reading?" I asked.

"This is my diary from college. I found it in my closet. It has everything. The first day of school, the first time I met my friend Cele, the first time I met your father…"

Abuelo drummed his fingers on the arm of his chair. Pingüino poked me in the shoulder.

"Quit stalling, Adela. Do you have anything or not?"

"I –"

Papi's door creaked open and he walked past the living room into the kitchen without so much as glancing at us. He went to the fridge and opened it. We avoided looking at him. He got out the plastic gallon of Abuelo's coconut water and poured it in a glass before sitting in the center of the couch, alone.

"Do you mind if I have some?" Papi said to Abuelo.

Abuelo shook his head with his eyes at his lap, "No, not at all."

There was a knocking on the door, a beating of fists, and it startled us. Papi got up to answer and his glass of coconut water spilled onto the floor. When he opened the door, Celia collapsed through it.

"Celia?" I said.

"*Ay Dios*, here we go again," Abuelo said.

Celia was on her knees and her body was shaking. She wore the same outfit she had worn that day at the shoe shop – the fuzzy off-the-shoulder top, and the skirt with the slit in it, and the high heels. Her top was ripped at the shoulder and it flapped like a piece half-peeled skin. Her teeth were smothered thickly in blood. There was a bruise forming at her cheek, and another on her neck, and another on her arm. Another one lidded Celia's left eye shut like a rotten grape.

"Help me, for God's sake."

Papi yanked her up by the arm and shook her.

"I told you not to come back here!" he screamed.

"Don't touch her that way," Mami snapped. "Can't you see she's hurt?"

Papi let go and Celia fell to the floor crying.

"This wasn't supposed to happen, this was never supposed to happen," Celia sobbed.

"Adela, help her to the couch please," Mami said. She was already in the kitchen, wetting a rag.

"What? Are you serious?" Pingüino asked.

"Yes, I'm serious."

I hesitated before touching her because I didn't know how to grab her, and I didn't know where to touch her so it wouldn't hurt. When I did, her skin was warm, but she pulled away and staggered to her feet. She sat in the middle of the couch where Papi had been.

"What happened?" Papi asked, nearing her.

"I'm sorry to have come here, I couldn't think of anywhere else," Celia said, and she latched onto him. "I'm sorry, I'm so sorry..."

"Celia —"

"I told him — I told him I didn't want to and he just — *Ay Dios, Jesús, Santa María, perdónenme* —"

"Here," Mami said, handing her the wet rag. Celia held it to her face and a strand of bloodstained saliva dribbled down her chin.

"Dulce told me, she told me it would happen to me too if I stayed but I never thought — I thought I could get away —"

"Celia," Papi said, "What *happened?*"

"He..." Celia gulped, her eyes darting to where me and Pingüino were huddled. I was aware of the scent of coconut juice in the air, of the anger building in Papi's eyes, of Pingüino's trembling lips, of the glare of Abuelo's glasses, of the faint resentment in the way Mami regarded Celia's wine-dark skin. "He raped me."

Pingüino's forehead crinkled and I could tell he didn't know what the word meant. I dreaded to think of how things would change when he did. Papi's face was smooth and still.

"Who did it?" Papi said.

"There's nothing you can do."

"Where is he?"

"He'll kill you."

"I don't care."

"Yes, you do. He'll kill anyone who ever mattered to you."

"Who is he?"

"I'm not telling you."

"Is he one of your clients?"

"Yes."

"You tried to quit didn't you?"

"Yes."

"It's my fault."

"No, it's not. I want to quit and it's not your fault."

"Did you want to quit because of me?"

"Yes."

"Then it's my fault."

"There's nothing you could have done."

"There's plenty I could have done," Papi said, and he met Mami's eyes over Celia's shoulder. He refocused on Celia's face. "I can do something now."

"You can't."

Papi snarled and grabbed her wrist. Celia yelped and her hand turned a dead ash-grey.

"Tell me where he is!"

"Sebastián, stop it!" Mami said. "Why don't we call the police?"

"No," Celia said, shaking her head. "The police never believe us. It happened to someone I know once, and they don't – they never –"

"Let me fix it, Celia."

"You *can't!*"

"Let go of her, Sebastián."

"I'm not letting him get away with it. What if it were Adela?"

"But you can't just –"

"Tell me!"

"No!"

Papi squeezed her wrist and Celia screamed. The windows must have shaken. Abuelo covered his ears with his hands.

"*Por Dios*, stop hurting her like that!" Abuelo said.

"Where is he?"

"The Hotel Nacional."

"What room?"

"211."

Papi strode towards the door.

"Where are you going?" Mami said.

"I'm going to find the bastard and pull the hair out of his scalp if he has any."

"Why don't we tell Rodrigo? He'll do something."

"No. This is for me to do. *Adiós*, Deianeira."

Celia screamed, "He'll kill you! He'll kill you all!"

Papi closed the screen door. The headlights of Abuelo's car lit up. They rushed away, as innocent as fireflies in the dark, past the windows and the curtains and the paint-chipped houses of Marianao. And I had no trouble imagining those headlights traveling up the driveway in Vedado that was lined with palm trees, pulling up next to the limousines and the sleek black cars. I could see it all – the reds and whites and yellows of the lobby with its glass sliding doors and its fancy suitcases and its bellhops, and *los americanos* who didn't know of Papi in his blue old man's car with death in his heart for whoever happened to be in room 211, or of Miguel who had almost been blown to pieces there a few weeks before.

Celia wiped her eyes, and was small in the indent Papi had left in the couch.

"I should never have come here," she said, "He's as good as dead."

Pingüino picked up the dominoes and I helped him, both of us on our knees, coconut water soaking into my dress. I found Papi's glass and I righted it on the carpet, though it was empty now. We found the box (the top of it had the Cuban flag etched into the lid) and placed in the dominoes one by one, stacked up like a pile of yellowed shining teeth. In the kitchen, Mami muttered to herself about bandages. Abuelo went to the television and turned the volume up with a twist of the knob, where a newsman talked about the weather (*"Mañana, un poco de lluvia con temperaturas en los ochentas..."*), and then sat in his chair.

As we slid the wooden lid over the dominoes, Celia watched the newsman on the television.

"He's as good as dead," she whispered, to herself this time, as if she were the only person in the room.

"I'm not stupid if that's what you're thinking."

I was scared she might've been talking to me (I had been gazing off toward the mantel at the picture of Mami on the front steps with her wedding dress, wondering where she kept it hidden), but it didn't take long for me to realize that she was talking to Mami, who was sitting in the chair across from Abuelo's. Abuelo had gone to try and put Pingüino to bed because it was getting late, and Mami didn't want him to stay up waiting for someone who might not come back. Celia took turns holding the wet rag to her lip and then to her eye. There were dark finger marks across her throat as if a ghost were choking her.

"I didn't say anything," Mami said.

"I know when someone's judging me. It's part of my job. You think I'm stupid."

"I have nothing to say to you."

"Deianeira —"

"Don't call me that."

"What?"

"Call me Señora Santiago."

"Is it because of my skin?"

"*What?*"

"That you think I'm stupid."

Mami stared at her.

"You can admit it, if you like. I think it helps. Well, sometimes. For example: I think you are repressed and judgmental."

"*Por Dios*, is your sole purpose in life to make everyone around you uncomfortable?"

"Someone's got to do it. Otherwise, there's no truth."

Mami buried her head in her hands. "Why did this have to happen to me?"

"I don't know."

"The question was rhetorical."

"I hate those. They never have any answers."

"What is wrong with you?"

"People have been asking me that a lot lately."

"You're awfully calm."

"I'm really not, you know. I can feel my heartbeat in my breath, and I don't" – Celia took a deep breath – "I don't know how to *be* right now."

Mami sighed. She gazed at the floor for a long while before speaking. She looked haggard and defeated. "I don't know what to do either," she said, "He's going to get arrested or worse. I don't even know how this happened."

Celia was silent, gazing at the floor also.

"Who did this to you?" Mami said.

"The less you know the better."

"Is he a policeman?"

"No. He's a mobster. An American."

"This is going to ruin everything."

We watched the television uselessly.

"If he's a client," I said, "then why…?"

"Why did I say no?" Celia said, finishing my sentence. She wasn't surprised. I could tell Mami was disturbed I'd asked.

"Because I don't want this anymore. I got into it because when my parents died, me and Dulce were seventeen and fifteen and we needed jobs. We'd been sleeping in our Titi Sandra's Laundromat, but then Titi Sandra died and we needed money. I had always had some interest in it, because you see those women lounging around in the streets in their outfits smoking and some of them are just so ugly and you wonder 'How could anyone want that? Who could ever want that?' And after a few years, I could understand it. I've come to understand that some of those women are the most beautiful things in this whole city. But Dulce hated it. She hated it so much, and eventually she got to not liking me so much either. Eventually one of Dulce's clients got too rough with her one night, and she quit. Lucky for her she got that job at the Zapatería de Cuba, otherwise she might've cracked. I've never searched for another job because I was okay with myself. But then I met your father and I wanted someone to think I was special. These last few weeks there's been no joy in this work. And the man who did this to me, he's been using me for years, every time he comes to the city. Except this time I didn't want to and I told him I didn't want to but he wouldn't listen and he just kept saying '*Dale dale* it's okay, gorgeous, Imma take care of you, gorgeous' but I told him no and he just..."

And then she wasn't calm anymore and she started crying again.

"I'm sorry," she said. "I'm so sorry."

"Celia," I said. "Are you saying Dulce was...?"

Celia nodded.

"And you were fifteen when you started?"

Celia nodded again.

"How old are you exactly?" Mami asked, and there was no tenderness in her voice.

Celia chuckled, and the sound of it was ugly through the tears, "There you go. I said it, didn't I? Judgmental. To the core."

I felt bad for her. She had no one. She didn't have a mother or an aunt or a sister to wrap their arms around her as she wept. And I could almost see how she could convince herself that someone like Papi might love her, to save her from having to return alone to her sagging old mattress and her decrepit gray building with laundry lines fluttering out the window. I wished she had someone other than Mami whose eyes held no sympathy, and me whose arms would never be enough, and how could they with what she'd been through?

And yet she had ruined everything. I knew she was young and naïve and probably didn't know any better, but still I was mad at the way things had played out, and I understood now how Señora Valle could feel so helpless and angry at the same time about the things she couldn't control. I couldn't even understand how Papi had picked Celia over Mami, how he could ignore the life they had built and choose Celia instead. Then there was Celia herself. Impulsive and selfish and stupid all at once. She had had the nerve to barge into our house twice and look Mami in the eye and demand that the world align itself for her, and here was the result. Mami, Celia, and I together in the half-light waiting for the world to fall apart. Papi in Abuelo's car traveling to Vedado in the nighttime.

I thought about what Miguel had said, about how the mobsters at the Hotel Nacional didn't have their guns with them, and I hoped to God it was true. Abuelo came back and the exhaustion in his eyes told us how things had gone with Pingüino. He returned to his green chair and I sat on the arm of it. Soon a tortuous hour had passed, and I realized that it was Miguel and the Hotel Nacional all over again, except this time it was Papi and it was all Celia's fault. My eyes felt heavy, but I pinched myself on the shoulder every time I felt myself drifting. Celia cried sometimes, and in the more quiet moments stared vacantly at the wall, perhaps thinking of the suffering she had caused, although I didn't think so. Abuelo fell asleep and I moved to the chair next to Mami, her college diary gleaming on her lap. On the television, a telenovela played, but none of us watched. We let the light wash over our faces, knowing we were all thinking the same thing: *Why isn't he back yet?*

Papi lying dead in the street between the cobblestones.

*Why isn't he back yet?*

Papi bullet-ridden, his corpse floating in the turquoise pool.

*Why isn't he back yet?*
Papi with his throat slit, his neck bleeding into the pillow.
*Why isn't he back yet?*
Or...
*Stop it,* I told myself.
12:30. A key clattering in the lock. My heartbeat pulsed in my throat. Mami grabbed hold of my hand and she was quivering. The door creaked open.

Papi. Stone-faced. A splatter of red on his shirt. His fists hung at his sides, and they were bruised like the knuckles of the stranger who'd punched Luis. He said nothing. Celia stood. Abuelo snored, glasses askew. Everyone stared at one another. Then Mami tackled him with a hug, and he took it, wrapped his arms around her, and stroked the back of her hair with his eyes shut, maybe because otherwise he would have cried and there had been enough crying in our house over the past few days. Mami pulled away and remembered to be angry. She smacked him in the arm and screamed, "What did you do? Are you hurt? I can't believe –"

Celia lingered by the couch, uncomfortable with herself.

"Is he dead?" she said.

"No."

"That was stupid of you."

"I didn't want to kill him."

"He won't leave you alone. His cars will be up and down this street within the next few days and one day you'll come home to the windows shattered. You have to run. Pack everything as fast as you can and get out of here. You can't tell your friends, you can't tell your neighbors. Just take everything and go. *Todo y todo el mundo.* Everything and everyone."

My stomach dropped. *Everything.* Everything was falling apart. I tried thinking about all those things I had ever known, all those things I would have to say good-bye to. But I couldn't. It was just a white buzzing, a big blank. And in that big white buzzing blank,

Celia's words rebounded and cascaded and grew louder and softer over and over again – *todo, todo, todo, everything, everything, everything…*

"You can't be serious," Mami said, and something told me she knew of the big white buzzing blank also, could hear it crumbling all around her shoulders, "Everything? How do you know?"

"I've known him long enough to understand how he works. You have to get out of Havana by the end of the week."

"Won't he follow us?"

"He's an American. To him Havana is all there is of Cuba – his whorehouse, his casino, his cigars, his rum, his five-star hotel. He won't stray far."

Mami was pale like she wanted to throw up in the sink, "Where will we go?"

"Anywhere," Celia said.

"I'll send a letter to Noelia at the plantation," Papi said. "I'll tell her to be ready in a week."

"Oriente?"

"We need to get away from here."

"But that's where Fidel is. That's where the rebellion is. I've seen it in the papers. And what about Pingüino and Adela? Don't think there are any schools there I'd send them to, and… Sebastián, we've been here so long. So long I can't remember having been anywhere else. How can we leave?"

"You're going to have to," Celia said.

"Oh, why did you have to do it?" Mami cried.

"What's done is done," Papi said.

"But you didn't even think." It slipped out of my mouth quiet and soft. I barely knew it existed. The whole room paused. Abuelo's snoring sifted in the air.

"What do you mean I didn't think?"

"You didn't think about us."

"Adela –"

"You lied when you said you loved Mami, didn't you?"

"What?"

"You don't care about her. You don't care about any of us."

Papi was speechless.

"What about me and Pingüino? Were we never enough?"

"Of course, you're enough, you were always —"

"No we weren't. We never were. We were just some more things to ignore, some more things to destroy."

"How can you say that?"

Suddenly the big white buzzing blank snapped into place, and it came to me, the world I would have to say goodbye to. Me and Pingüino sitting on the wall of el Malecón with the waves crashing behind us. We were old and wrinkled like Abuelo and we ate popcorn by the sea. The sky was red and pink and orange all at once like layers of sherbert the way it always was at sunset in Havana, the way it had been our whole lives. We had grown up in our small blue house in Marianao and gone to school at the University of Havana and married and had children and our grandchildren played on the cobblestone of the walkway, feeding the pigeons. There were teenagers drinking wine from cartons on the sidewalks and old African ladies selling rosaries from booths. It came to me so vividly, the Havana of my mind. I could taste the salt of the popcorn burning my tongue, could smell the heavy sweat-scent of ocean. That Havana was ours and it would always be ours, except it wasn't. It wasn't and it never could be, and I realized that it wasn't just things I would have to say goodbye to, but an entire future, an entire possibility of life I could have had if it weren't for Papi. He had taken his boredom and dissatisfaction and plunged blind into his so-called survival and in the process he had rerouted our lives. I was crying and I hadn't even realized it, "I hate you."

Papi's eyes dimmed, and there was a long silence. He opened his mouth a few times to speak, but didn't. He had run out of ways to justify himself. Papi stared at his own hands and blinked. Then he walked away.

"Where are you going?" Mami said.

"To take a shower."

"But what do we do?"

"We'll pack in the morning," Papi said, then disappeared into the hallway.

"I'm staying," Celia said, "I want to help." And even though I realized it wasn't all her fault and that it never could be, I hated the fact she was still here and that she had spoken.

"Fine," Mami said, "I'm not in control anyway. We'll deal with this in the morning. Celia, you can sleep on the couch if you want. My father will probably get up in the middle of the night and wander back to his room, so don't worry about him and…" Mami sighed as if she couldn't believe she had to say it to her husband's mistress in her own living room filled with her furniture, and the pictures of her children, and all the things she had accumulated over the past thirteen years… "*Buenas noches*, Celia."

"*Buenas noches*, Señora Santiago."

Celia picked up the bloody rag and it unpeeled itself from the floor with a wet squelch. She began washing it in the sink. The dripping of the water echoed in the night. Mami hugged me and wiped the tears from my cheeks.

"In the morning a new day," she told me, "As for your father messing up the beautiful things in life, the only advice I can give you is…" She glanced at Celia who was wringing water from the towel, and whispered it like a secret, "*Never get married.*"

Three days. That's all it took. Our entire lives in Marianao packaged in a mere eight boxes. We piled them by the front door so that when night fell, we'd carry them to Abuelo's car, one by one, so the neighbors wouldn't talk. It wasn't everything. Just the essentials. Mami's pots and pans with the brown grizzle on the bottoms. Pingüino's old baseball bat. Papi's piggy bank that his father gave him when he'd gone off to college. Rubia, my stuffed bunny with the pink ribbon Tía Carmen had given me as a baby.

All of the pictures on the dresser were swept up at once, piled into a box along with a few odds and ends; Pingüino's baby shoes, our childhood drawings, Mami's diary from college. Mami wanted to take the lamp, but Papi wouldn't let her. Then, clothing for everyone. Papi's church clothes and Mami's yellow flower print dress that smelled of oldness. Me and Pingüino's school uniforms though we knew deep down, as we folded them and rubbed out the creases, that we would never use them, or any other school uniform, ever again. A pair of shoes for each of us, all of them made in Papi's shop. We picked them based on memory rather than convenience. All of the furniture was to be left behind, including Abuela's old dressing table and Abuelo's green armchair. Mami's makeup was to be left in the drawers, Papi's heavy dress suit in the closet.

Celia stayed in the house all three days, and every day she stood in the living room, piling stuff into sections and helping Mami decide what got to stay and what got to go. It was surreal watching them work together. I expected Mami to explode any moment, but she seemed to have accepted things. On the first day, Celia had these two determined creases in her chin, and she pretended as if her clothes weren't torn, her lip wasn't cut, her hair wasn't a mess. The two of them in the living room, passing things around, one after the other, like an assembly line. And me and Pingüino would help wordlessly hours on hours on end after school, because Papi said that pulling us out might be "suspicious" and people might "start to wonder what was going on."

At Tío Rodrigo's house, things were just the same. Sometimes me and Pingüino went over to their house to help, and they had even fewer things to pack up than we did. Tía Carmen had her collection of old mint cans in the cabinet above the bathroom sink that we persuaded her to throw away. Tío Rodrigo had his police certification in an old glass frame, the paper on the inside filled with indecipherable cursive and a faded coffee ring on the bottom right corner. Miguel packed all of his things up within two hours, in an old suitcase of his father's whose zippers got stuck midway through.

Miguel had been thinking about what he would pack for a long time: "All I need are my hot posters of Elizabeth Taylor, my baseball stuff, a few changes of clothes, and a few bottles of Coca-Cola. Everything else can burn for all I care. Adela, I'll admit that Tío Sebastián cheating on Tía Deianeira is about the worst thing I've ever heard of. But I can't tell you how happy I am to get out of this neighborhood. I'm tired of walking down the streets scared of bombs and guns on the way to work. I want to get away from the Hotel Nacional and its stupid smiling *americanos*. And now that I know that one of them's the reason we've got to clear out, I'm not sorry if I can put miles between me and that place... There are some things we'll miss though, won't we? Like riding our bikes and talking about crazy Luis Rodriguez... I suppose we'll never know what happened to those kids who disappeared. Or who threw those bombs at me in the first place... Oh, well. Maybe wherever we're going there'll be plenty of *chicas hermosas*, pretty girls to go after, eh? There certainly aren't any in this town, I'll tell you that. It's not like I haven't searched."

As for Pingüino, things had been rough. Night after night, it was conversations of "Will they ever love each other again?" and "Why is Celia still here? Why do they let her stay?" and sometimes barely any words at all. Just the both of us lying flat on our backs, counting down the hours we had left in this place, in this bedroom, the only place we'd ever slept in our entire lives. And even with everything going on, Havana and Marianao bustled on. There were still gunshots pop-pop-popping at night, though we were no longer as scared of them. There were still people getting the groceries. There was still Señora Rodriguez waving to us whenever she saw us, and Señor Moreno smoking log-like cigars from the comfort of his front porch. Papi still shined his shoes in the mornings. Mami still cleaned the dishes and did the laundry. Abuelo still sat in his green chair and watched television.

One day, I noticed Abuelo standing sad in a corner, observing as everything was dismantled. Celia and Mami had taken a quick fifteen-minute break to drink glasses of water that sweat in the heat, and soon they were back at it, cleaning out the contents of the kitchen cabinets this time – old cans of beans and rusted whisks and the pan Mami had used to make a turkey one Christmas a couple of years ago. And Abuelo did nothing but watch. Half his body was disappearing into the curtains, white with green stenciling. I half expected them to swallow him whole, for him to vanish in a pale swish of fabric.

"Abuelo. What are you thinking?"

Abuelo sighed, and rubbed his eyes beneath his glasses. The tips of his fingers, when he took them away, were wet. "About how hard it is to build things up. And how easy it is to tear them apart."

He touched his hands to the curtains as if he expected them to stay put, but they floated away, just out of reach. The sunlight dappled them into ghosts.

"Your *abuela* made these curtains three weeks before she died," Abuelo said. "She was too skinny for her favorite dress at the end. Before she got sick, she used to wear it all the time, with these white pair of sandals that were so worn on the bottoms the soles were peeling off."

A tear dribbled onto his cheek. He continued as if it hadn't happened, and let it quiver there as he talked. "When she cut it up, the whole house was so quiet, you could hear every snip of the scissors. She could hardly use her fingers to sew the fabric together, they were shaking so much, but she was determined to be done with that old thing. Taunting her in the closet every morning about the way she used to be. The first time seeing the bits of dress hung up by the window, it was like seeing a dead animal hung up to dry. Like Adela had strung a bit of herself up there to die before the rest of her did."

Abuelo took a bunch of curtain, and held it tightly in his fist, making deep, violent creases.

"I don't want to leave you behind, Adela." His voice broke. "I don't want to. But I have to. You won't be happy in the countryside, and I couldn't do that to you. I won't move you, I won't."

The blood rushed through my head. "Me?"

"No, I mean her. Her."

He stared vacantly at the white-and-green fabric. "*Mi Adela, mi pobre Adela...*"

25 As Meaningless as Shoes

In all the time we spent packing, I only saw Papi and Celia together once. They were on the front porch and the sun was setting. Mami was dealing with the porcelain and I was helping her pack it all into boxes with leftover tissue paper from the shoe shop, the kind of paper that was used to package shoes. The table in the kitchen had been moved to make more room, and we were sitting on the floor with bits of paper scattered all about. The orange of the walls reflected the light of the sunset and it bounced around the room and settled onto the paper as if we were stranded in a valley of orange peels.

"Are you sure we have to pack this?" I asked.

"Yes," Mami said. "I spent a lot of money on it."

"I know. I wanted some *pastelitos* from the Panadería and you bought dusty old porcelain from the antique shop instead."

Mami laughed. "And your father was furious with me for buying them, but we put them to good use anyway, didn't we? All those Christmas Eves…" She wrapped a cup with a chip in it and put it at the bottom of the box.

"Mami," I said. "How can you be okay with this?"

"With what?"

"All of this."

"You mean your father?"

I nodded. She pursed her lips. "I'm not sure I am."

"Mami, I think I really hate him."

"Don't say that."

"But it's true."

"No, it isn't. Even I don't hate him."

"You don't?"

"No."

"You've forgiven him?"

"No, it's not that either. It's more that I've let go. I was sad at first about leaving, but then again I wasn't very happy here. I don't think life in Oriente will be so bad. I might even dance again."

"Really?"

"Really."

"What about school? You said you wouldn't let us go."

"No, but I'll teach you. Both of you. There'll be more people at the plantation anyway, more people to do the jobs I used to do. I think it's time other people did some of the cooking for a change."

"You mean no more *ropa vieja?*"

"No, I'll make it for you, Dela. But it'll be because I want to."

"I still hate him."

"No, you don't. You'll see."

"Can I take a break?"

"Sure. But don't take too long. There are still things to do."

I walked into the living room, and that's when I saw them. Papi and Celia on the front porch. The sight of them made something inside me recoil because I couldn't believe they could be so stupid after everything that had happened to continue speaking to each other. They were sitting on the top step together, and Celia had the white box between them, the white box with the red shoes. The door was propped open and I could hear them speaking quietly.

"But I thought you wanted them?" Papi said.

"I did, but I don't anymore. They're beautiful."

"I want you to keep them. They're yours."

"I know, it's just…"

"What?"

"I don't need a reminder."

"It's not your fault, you know. It's mine."

"No, it's his. Not us. Him."

"Won't he come after you?"

"He won't. It's fine."

"How do you know?"

"I don't know. I just... do. He cares for me in his own way, I think. Trust me."

"How can you say that after what he did to you?"

"I – I don't know. Please, I don't want to talk about it anymore."

A pause.

"You can come with us if you like," Papi said.

Celia hesitated. "There's no room in the car."

"You can take the train. That's how my brother and his family are getting out."

"No one will want me where you're going. The best thing for me to do is forget, and I can't do that if you don't take the shoes back."

"Please, Celia. Keep them."

Celia searched Papi's face. "I can't have them."

"Yes, you can. I want you to have them."

"Please, I –"

"No. You're keeping them. Not because you want to, but because I'm asking you to. Here." Papi placed the box in her lap.

She placed her hands on the box and stared at her fingers. "Okay," she said finally. "I'll keep them... But only because they won't mean anything. They'll be shoes and nothing more."

Papi gazed at her sadly. "Of course."

"When are you leaving?"

"The day after tomorrow. Early in the morning."

"Haven't you finished packing?"

"Yes, but I need to find someone to take care of the shoe shop, and my brother needs to get his last paycheck from the police department. Then we leave."

"Oh."

"Will you be there?"

"What?"

"Will you be there to say goodbye?"

"I don't think that's a good idea."

"Tomorrow night. Just to say good-bye."

"Sebastián..."

"Please."

Celia sighed and stared at the sky. "Fine. But no funny business. Just good-bye and nothing more. As meaningless as the shoes."

"As meaningless as the shoes," Papi agreed.

Celia replaced the lid on the box with the shoes in it. She stood. "Goodbye, Sebastián Santiago."

"This isn't goodbye. Tomorrow is."

"I know, but for now it is. Goodbye." She kissed him on the cheek. She stepped off the porch. She walked away. Past Rafi Consuelo's house and Señor Moreno's house and the intersection between them. Past the allamanda bush and the spot where the dog had died with its eyes rolling the year before. She kept walking until she was a speck in the distance and then she turned into oblivion.

After Celia left, night blushed its darkness across the sky, a thimble-full of silver pinpricks bleeding their way through. Miguel, Pingüino, and I had never gathered on the front porch at night, but I suppose it didn't matter anymore. This first would be our last. We had cleared out everything from the refrigerator except for a gallon of milk, and Mami told us we had to get rid of it. So we put it on the top step, taking swigs from it and not bothering with cups. We drank from it silently, like family.

The mosquitoes were out. They bit at us every few minutes, and every few minutes one of us would smack ourselves hard across the bumps forming on our arms and legs. I got a mosquito bite the size of a coin at the base of my index finger and I scratched it until it bled.

"Did Tío Rodrigo tell you why the two strangers were arrested?" I asked Miguel.

"No. He doesn't talk about work. He told us he'd arrested them, but he wouldn't give us their names or why they'd been arrested. Things have gotten worse since then. He's more nervous, and he comes in late more often. More panic attacks in the bathroom. Let's just say it's hard to find somewhere to take a piss nowadays."

"Panic attacks?" Pingüino asked.

Miguel nodded, and didn't explain. He took a swig from the gallon of milk.

"I never told you guys about the last time I saw Luis Rodriguez, did I?" I said.

"No!" Pingüino said, "No, you did *not* tell us about the last time you saw Luis Rodriguez. When was this? *Por Dios*, Adela you've been holding out on us."

"I'm with Pingüino on this one," Miguel said, "Spill the beans, *prima*."

"Well, I went over there on Sunday after... you know, after the first time Celia came to the house. It was while everyone else was at church, and you, Pingüino, were sleeping, no help at all, and I went over there to return the cups and spoons we'd taken from Señora Rodriguez's house the week before. Luis opened the door and he was in pretty bad shape – had this big bruise on his cheek and a gash on his forehead. He told me it was those two strangers who'd done it. And then he said all these weird things like 'Forgive me' and 'I did the right thing' and 'Do you like President Batista?' Then he grabbed me and told me he regretted nothing. So I ran out of there as fast as I could."

Another mosquito bit my neck, and I smacked at it.

"Jesus, Adela," Miguel said. "And you forgot to mention this?"

I shrugged. "A lot of things happened after that with Celia. I forgot."

"Like I said," Pingüino huffed, "All the fun stuff happens to Adela."

"It wasn't fun at all. He could've done anything to me and no one would've known. He could've slit my throat and buried me under the lemon trees and that would've been the end of it."

"Stop being so melodramatic," Pingüino said, "I know he's creepy and that there's a good chance he's a *rebelde*, but I don't think he'd do something like that..." Miguel was uncertain in the dark. "Would he?"

Miguel took another swig from the gallon of milk. "It doesn't matter. We won't ever know. By the end of the week, we'll be far away and never coming back."

"*Dios mío*, you say that like it's a good thing," Pingüino said, "Aren't you even a little bit sad?"

"Nope."

"I can't believe it's happening," I said. "I keep seeing all the boxes piled into the back of Abuelo's car, and it feels like we're going on vacation somewhere and we'll be back soon. Like we're just going to the beach for a few days, packing up towels and swimsuits and extra clothes and sandals and getting sand all over the car, but we'll be back. But we're not. We're leaving. Forever."

"Hmm," Pingüino said. He gazed at the pinpricks in the sky. I could see a mosquito bite the shape of a torpedo on his elbow. He took the jug of milk and tried swigging it like Miguel had. Except he tilted it too far and it spewed everywhere. Milk squirted out of Pingüino's mouth and it sounded like the air being let out of a balloon too fast. "*¡COJONES!*" he screamed, and me and Miguel laughed.

"It's not funny!" Pingüino said. He grabbed his nose and his voice came out nasally, "*Ay, mierda*, I think some of it went up my nose."

We laughed so hard tears poured down our cheeks. Miguel kept pounding his fist on the top step of the porch, struggling for breath.

"I could have died!" Pingüino cried. "Would you be laughing then?"

"Yes," I said, wheezing.

And me and Miguel we laughed in a way we hadn't laughed in a long time – the last time had been when Miguel told us the story of when he'd been trying to flirt with some French girl on el Paseo del Prado in Havana. She was brunette, wore big sunglasses in the shape of butterfly wings, spoke snatches of Spanish with guttural French Rs, and was drop-dead gorgeous, and he'd farted by accident while telling her how she reminded him of the sun. We laughed then like we laughed now. Until our faces were red and the air in our lungs had been leaked out, and we were reduced to weak giggling, stranded like beached fish on the steps of the porch.

Pingüino had gone still. The milk jug was abandoned at the top step. "Adela. Miguel."

His voice snagged at me, and I stopped laughing. There was an odd catch to it.

"What?" I said. "What is it?"

"There," Pingüino said, and he pointed behind us. "Tell me you see it too."

Miguel and I turned.

The lights in Rafi Consuelo's house were blazing again. I waited for them to snap out of existence like last time, but they wouldn't. They went on shining as if they knew we were watching and wouldn't settle for being predictable.

"I see it," Miguel said. "I actually see it."

"Ha!" Pingüino said. But there was a lilting uncertainty in his voice as he said it. "I saw it first!"

"*Cállate*, Pingüino," I said, "What do we do?"

"I'll tell you what we do," Miguel said. He stood. "We're going over there."

"Are you crazy?" I said, "I thought you were okay with not knowing."

"Yes. That's what I said when I thought we'd never know. But the lights are on again, Adela. It's now or never. Either we go over there or we never know. Is that what you want?"

"But what about the police? Or Tío Rodrigo? Shouldn't we tell them?"

"Come on, we know what happens then. The lights go out, the police take over, and we never know. Or they lie about it. Do you really think everything they say in the newspapers is true? Aren't you sick of the lies, Adela? All the lies and the things we've got to keep inside, the things we can't say out loud. Just once, Adela, I'd like to be free. Let's be free. The three of us together. What do you say?"

"I don't think this is a good idea, Miguel."

"And what about you Pingüino? In or out?"

Pingüino drew himself up taller. His shirt was soaked in milk, and some of it clung to his face, "In."

"Please, Adela," Miguel said.

I studied Rafi Consuelo's house and the blaring white glow behind the curtains. No more lies. No more secrets. Just take the house apart wall by wall until it was rooms and furniture and picture frames and whoever stood inside flicking light switches on and off, stranded in the open. We would be eyes in the sky, peering in through the rooftops.

"I'll do it," I said.

Together, we stepped away from the familiar circle of yellow alley-light glow that embraced our porch every night. Together, we barreled into the mosquito-filled darkness, on toward the whiteness flooding from Rafi Consuelo's resurrected house.

Rafi Consuelo's doorknob was rusted, and we stared at it, daring each other to be the first to touch it, but no one would. Rafi Consuelo had a doormat and it was soaked with old rain, squelching beneath our feet as we shifted back and forth. It was the same night, the same darkness, the same white-glow behind Rafi Consuelo's shutters. But it felt different on this side of things. Right there in front of us. A twist of the doorknob away.

The lights went out.

"*Coño,* did you see that?" Pingüino said.

"Shhh!" Miguel said, "What if someone hears you?"

There was a tightness in my chest. I tried the doorknob. It was old and rusted. It grated as it gave, and the door swung open into empty air. A hush fell over us and, one by one, we stepped in. Miguel first. Pingüino second. Me last. We blinked in the dark, our eyes creating shapes out of layers of shadow. Then a face loomed from the dark.

"Close the door."

"Rafi, is that you?" Pingüino said, rubbing his eyes.

"Close the damn door right now."

Objects in the room took form one by one. First, the walls adorned with street art, the kind tourists bought – pictures of beaches and palm trees, and sexy showgirls shaking maracas, and women with flowers in their hair. Then the floors came into view. They were covered in crumpled newspapers with headlines from weeks before ("Batista Smashes Armed Revolt," "Bomb Goes Off on the Grounds of Hotel Nacional") along with old cigar butts and half-blackened matchsticks and mostly empty glasses of rum, some of it spilled sticky and old at the corner of the room, a swarm of ants swimming half-dead. The next thing was the patched-up couch that could have only belonged to a college student, to someone who had found it on the side of a highway exit somewhere. Then – what was on the couch and scattered around it.

I counted five machine guns. Sleek and shining, but peaceful in the way they were tossed on the ground, slung over the back of the couch by their straps like women's purses. More than a dozen rifles also, too many to count, with broad wooden bases leaning against the back wall. The handguns were in a haphazard pile, four of them, nested atop a bundle of clothing I recognized as Havana police uniforms, their bright blue stranded on the floor oddly – as if pieces of noonday sky had unpeeled themselves from the heavens and fallen to earth. And then, rounds and rounds of ammunition. Gold-headed and linked together, each one a miniature of Mami's tubes of red lipstick. Great strings of them laid out on the couch, deadly Christmas garlands meant to be wrapped around a tree, garrote-like.

And after all that – after the posters, the crumpled newspapers, the cigarettes, the matchsticks, the old rum, the battered couch, the weapons shining sinister in starlight – was the face itself, the one that had spoken. Its glasses. Its awkward black mustache. The nervous fidgetiness of its eyes. It was a man and he was pointing a handgun at my chest.

"Luis?"

"*Hola* Adela," Luis Rodriguez said.

"What is all this?"

"Fidel, of course," Luis said, and he sounded bitter, "What did you think it was?"

A moment of silence as we absorbed everything – the room, the weapons, Luis Rodriguez, the very real gun pointed at us.

Pingüino's grip tightened around my fingers, and I feared the tips of my fingers might be blue.

"The Presidential Palace," Miguel said. "That was you wasn't it?"

"What? No."

"Then what are all these weapons for?"

"It's a weapons cache. Not the only one in the city, I might add."

"Did you kill Rafi and Anita?"

"No, I didn't do any of that."

"Then what did you do?" I said.

"I've made a horrible mistake."

"I thought you said you did the right thing."

"I know. I was trying to convince myself through you and I'm sorry about that. I let them get to my head, and I shouldn't have."

"I don't know what you're talking about. Luis, please let us go. We won't tell anyone, we promise. We'll just leave this house, and you can leave the lights off and no one will ever know, okay? Can you – Can you put down the gun, please?"

"Adela, do you know what Cuba is?" he said, as if he hadn't heard me.

I kept my mouth shut.

"It's people dragging their lives behind them, but no one cares who's in charge. And if one day America or Batista or somebody decides to fuck with our city, turn streets into brothels, and have murderers run the economy, do you know what those people do? They go on. They go on and they pretend like nothing's happening and maybe – that's what they think in their heads – maybe things will turn out all right. Don't make a fuss and I can go on living, that's what they think. But what about everyone else? What about those shirtless kids in the slums by the baseball stadium? The ones who live under the lights of a casino sign? They don't have any life with which to go on living. What they get is hell, *la casa del carajo*. No one does anything and that's what Cuba is right now.

"Fidel… *por Dios* maybe you're too young to understand this, but Fidel knows. He knows what's wrong. He sees these people, these poor bastards banished to *la casa del carajo* for no good reason, and he wants to fix it. And in the beginning that's why I did what I did. *Los americanos* there lounging by their goddamn pool in their goddamn hotel because Havana is just their playhouse, because all they think we are are funny people speaking a funny language, and by God, I thought, by God they'd understand –"

"Wait," Miguel said. "That was you? You bombed the Hotel?"

"Are you Miguel?"

"Yes."

"I used to know you when I was younger. Maybe you don't remember. It was baseball. In the field by the Catholic School. You were so small you couldn't play yet, and I remember your mother used to yell at you because you liked running your hands through the dirt and getting your pants dirty."

Miguel was caught off guard for a moment, "You tried to kill me."

"No, I didn't want to. I just – It was an idea I had. It was before coming here. It was me and Jorge and Pablo – the two men you met at church a few weeks ago – and we were on the train together coming back from the Sierra Maestra, from months and months of sweating in the jungles and learning how to shoot at people from far away and the train ride was just the three of us talking about *los americanos* and how they thought we were so small and how they went inside their spotless cages in hotels like the Hotel Nacional and refused to know about the suffering they caused. And how Batista loved those spotless cages so much, cradled them close to his heart, and sent all of his favorite rich people and mobsters and celebrities there like goddamn Frank Sinatra and goddamn Meyer Lanksy. And I said, I told them, 'Wouldn't it be great if we could teach them a lesson? Just bomb the place. Boom. Up in flames. That'd show them, wouldn't it?'

And we laughed about it for a bit, but then they got serious, and they talked about our weapons supply at Rafi Consuelo's and rounding up Anita Valle and having a University of Havana reunion, all of us. And if Rafi or Anita opted not to come, then we could just have the party without him. We got here and Rafi wasn't home. We sent a message to Anita, and no response. We thought maybe they'd gone out somewhere, so that night we decided we'd grab what we needed from Rafi Consuelo's, jump into Pablo's car, and throw the bomb over the side of the fence. At night. Poolside. *Los americanos cabrones* wouldn't know what had hit them. That's what we said. And that's what we did... But I understand now it was wrong. I could've hurt you, and the solution to no one trying to fix Cuba's mess isn't killing the people stuck dragging their lives behind them, because it isn't really their fault. They're just people trying to shoulder the daily burden. And the Americans too, they haven't done anything. They're ignorant, oblivious. The only thing those people at the Hotel Nacional are guilty of is not knowing, and it's a shame they don't know, but it's not their fault. It's not their fault at all. I used to think the way it should be done was to get rid of anyone who got in the way, because that's what they taught us in the mountains. If there's anyone in the way, get rid of them. Anyone is expendable. But... that night, that night at the Hotel Nacional, I could have killed so many people. That one moment, that bomb soaring in the air, was the worst mistake of my life. And I am sorry for that, Miguel. I truly am."

"There's something wrong with you," Miguel said. He was disgusted. "I can't even walk down the street anymore, Luis. It's all shadows and bombs and rebels to me and you did that. You. No one else. You're insane and I feel sorry for you. Sitting here in the dark, in the house of a man who's probably dead, flipping light switches and searching for forgiveness."

"Is that it?" Pingüino said, and I jumped because I'd forgotten he was there, because he was nothing but a sweaty palm grasping mine. "Is that why you turned on the lights?"

"Possibly," Luis said. His eyes were far away. His fingers tightened around the gun. "I didn't do it the first time. It was Jorge and Pablo, fumbling around like idiots and they turned the lights on by accident. They wanted to keep going. They wanted to go back to the Hotel and finish what they'd started. They saw it in the newspapers, and they didn't think it was good enough. They had a house full of weapons and they wanted to use them. I told them not to and I got beaten for it. They were arrested before they got the chance. Me? I was just sitting here in the dark in the middle of all this. And I thought someone ought to know. Someone ought to know before…"

"Before what?" I said.

Luis refocused, looked Miguel in the eyes.

"Miguel. I am a dead man because of you."

Luis raised the gun to his temple. He sucked in his breath through his teeth, about to shoot. Pingüino let go of my hand to cover his eyes.

"NO! LUIS, DON'T!" I screamed.

"Why not?" he said, and the tears streamed down his face.

"You didn't even hurt anyone!"

"I almost did. This is not who I thought I'd be. I thought I'd make things better, not worse."

"But that's not how it works, Luis! You said so yourself. It's never perfect and it never could be and it's better that way!"

"No, no," Luis sobbed, the gun pressed against his head.

"You want forgiveness, Luis? Forgive yourself."

"I can't," Luis whispered. "It's not that simple."

"It is, it is, I promise!"

"It's not just that I could have killed in the past, it's that I can kill in the future. You don't know what goes on in my head, the things I imagine. And it's more than that too. It's not just that I've failed in this, it's that I've failed in everything. All my mother does is sit in her house in her nightgown day after day. I've weighed her down her entire life. She might have been something and I ruined her. I have lived twenty-one years and I have nothing to show for it."

"Luis, please!"

"I'm sorry, Adela. I just... don't want to bother people anymore."

Pingüino had his hand clamped over his eyes and I could hear his breath shuddering in and out, in and out. Luis's finger trembled at the trigger.

"I forgive you." Miguel. His eyes down to the floor.

"What?"

"I forgive you."

Luis's mouth gaped and the tears made tracks alongside it. The tip of the gun was up against his forehead. Suddenly, blue and red lights. They washed across Luis's face, the walls, the couch, the weapons, the trash strewn across the floor. Outside the window, Tío Rodrigo's police car was parked on the street with its lights flashing.

"It's Tío Rodrigo," I said.

Pingüino uncovered his eyes, and Miguel peered out the window. Luis lowered the gun from his forehead, rushed towards us, and pushed us toward the back door. "Run — If they catch you here, they'll take you away and they'll do the same thing as... Lord knows what they're doing to them right now."

"Who?"

"All of them. Rafi and Anita. Jorge and Pablo."

"What? He's my uncle. He wouldn't do anything to us."

"Run," Luis opened the back door and pushed us into the night. "Hide if you have to. Don't let them see."

"But..." I said. "What about you?"

Luis's face was indecipherable in the dark. The gun gleamed in his hands.

"*Adiós*, Adela."
The door slammed shut.

All three of us trembled in the bushes. It was the allamanda bush with yellow flowers and green leaves taller than Abuelo's car, and all of it wet from a recent rain, brushing our cheeks and our arms and our hair with water droplets. On my right, Pingüino squatted slightly and his hair touched my shoulder. On my left, Miguel was behind me, his breath fluttering near my ear. We were dead quiet.

Tío Rodrigo clambered up the front steps, as skinny and frail as the last time we'd seen him. The golden center of his police cap shone. He knocked on the door to Rafi Consuelo's house. The police car was parked on the street and the lights were flashing. The houses up and down the street were unknowing of what went on outside, a few of them with lights behind closed curtains. Tío Rodrigo wasn't alone. Behind him was his partner, Manuel.

"Whoever you are," Tío Rodrigo said. "We know you're in there. Open the door."

He banged on the door. In the distance, a dog howled.

"Open up, or we'll force our way in. I'm giving you until the count of three."

"*Ay mierda, mierda, mierda,*" Miguel whispered in my ear. "Luis is still armed. What if he shoots? *Mierda,* he's going to shoot!"

"*¡UNO!*" Tío Rodrigo yelled. "*¡DOS!*" The door was immobile. "*…¡TRES!*"

They barged in and I put my fingers in my ears, waiting to hear pop-pop-popping, except this time it would be right in front of me rather than in a distant alley in Havana, or in the westerns Abuelo watched on the television. The world was muted, my fingernails digging into my ears. It hurt but I didn't care. A few seconds of blood pounding in my ears. Miguel's breath stopped fluttering by my neck. Pingüino had covered his eyes again with his hands.

Luis came out first. He was being pushed, he wasn't struggling. There was no gun. His hands were cuffed behind his back. Manuel held open the door of the police car, and I expected it to be quick and easy, for Tío Rodrigo to push him in, and we'd see the back of Luis's head and then he'd be driven away like the two strangers, perhaps with a tragic look through the back window as he wondered where those three kids went, the ones he'd threatened to kill himself in front of.

Instead – "Manuel, give me a moment. I need to ask Luis a few questions."

It was hard to see through the bushes, but I was pretty sure I saw Manuel raise his eyebrows. I could see the ends of his mustache, his canines a toothpaste-white in the darkness. I unplugged my ears.

"Please. He's my neighbor's son," Tío Rodrigo said.

Manuel hesitated, and then nodded. He retreated to the front seat of the police car. He rolled the windows up. Through the glass, I saw the orange beacon of a cigarette. Tío Rodrigo let go of Luis's arms, and Luis stood free by the back end of the police car, his wrists cuffed.

"You too, huh?" Tío Rodrigo said, "I'm terrified to think of what your mother will say tomorrow morning."

"I'm not expecting you to understand," Luis said. "Every few years there's a revolution and it gets crushed. But I'm telling you, Señor Santiago, this one will not be ignored. You haven't seen it. The base camps. Overflowing with men who are sick and tired of Batista's *mierda*. They'll come pounding into the rest of Cuba soon enough, and it won't be pretty for anyone when it does."

Tío Rodrigo shook his head. "You won't win, Luis. You've already lost."

"Tell me, Señor Santiago. How bad is it?"

"What?"

"The things they've been doing. To Rafi and Anita and Jorge and Pablo. How bad is it?"

"I don't know what you're talking about. Rafi and Anita have been missing for weeks and there's no sign of them."

Luis laughed. "*Por favor*. Do me the favor of telling me how I'm going to die."

Tío Rodrigo took off his policeman's hat to rub his head in the same way Papi ran his hands through his hair when he was nervous.

"Señor Santiago," Luis smiled. "There's no one here. It's just you and me and the night sky. And God, of course. My, what must he think of the both of us? Such moral dilemmas. It could take centuries for someone to contemplate them all, but thankfully He has time. And we can't forget Manuel smoking his cigarette in the front seat, although I don't think he can hear us, can he? Just you and me and God. I've been waiting for this, and I know what I'm going to do. I don't plan on talking. I don't plan on spilling. I plan on sitting there silent, screaming when I have to. Because I'm human and I can't help it. So you might as well tell me the truth. How painful is my death going to be?"

The rims of Tío Rodrigo's eyes were red. He sighed, and I recognized it. I recognized it as someone who was fed up with lying about things.

"Very," Tío Rodrigo said. His voice grated with truth. "It's going to be very painful."

"Let me go."

Tío Rodrigo glanced at Manuel's lit cigarette in the front seat. It was dimming fast. "I can't do that, Luis. I'm sorry."

"Do you want this? Do you want any more pain?"

"No. Of course not. I'm tired. So tired I can't breathe."

"Then let me go."

Luis Rodriguez faced the road that led to Señor Moreno's house, to the rusted mailboxes, to Havana and all of its white buildings and brothels and bars and restaurants and people and *americanos* and mobsters and citizens sleeping in the slums waiting to wake up to a new day. In his mind's eye, he must have seen the city's glow stretching all the way out to this suburb with its concrete porches and its crumbling streets. A future and a past he could never have. Not anymore.

Tío Rodrigo undid the cuffs. It was a smooth transaction. They faced each other as equals. Eye to eye. Chins up. The rebel and the cop. The mountains and the city. Fidel's soldier and Batista's enforcer. They shook hands on the battlefield, a good strong handshake. I could tell even from behind the leaves and the yellow flowers.

"Are you sure this is what you want?"

"I wasn't sure before," Luis said. I could've sworn Havana's glow rushed in his eyes, heavenly cars traveling on a freeway. "But I am now. I know what I want. I want to be let go."

Tío Rodrigo nodded. "Luis... I set you free."

No dogs barked in the night. No stray voices called from open kitchen windows. No gunshots drifted over from Havana. The light from Manuel's cigarette had gone out, and Manuel was a still, beautiful silhouette, a snapshot. The world was sucked in. Waiting. Patient. It could take its time on this one.

"Goodbye, Señor Santiago."

He faced Havana once more. He took a deep breath, and his shoulders moved with the exhalation. Then he ran. He ran so that his feet pounded pavement. I could feel the burning with him, the heat on my feet. I could feel the humidity part its way for me like ghosts. I could feel the cleanness of the air tunneling into my lungs, my chest. I could feel my clothes so light around me it was as if they weren't there at all. I was born again.

Tío Rodrigo removed the gun from his holster. He shot Luis Rodriguez three times and his figure crumpled, the blood across his back like three roses in bloom. On the ground he was a rag doll. One minute a man and the next a rag doll. Pingüino cried. A sharp breath outwards from Miguel. I was silent because I knew I was supposed to be.

After Manuel rushed out and got the story from Tío Rodrigo and saw the bloodstains on Luis Rodriguez's shirt, the two policemen piled into the car. They drove away, making a circle around the body as if they were afraid of waking it. And the three of us stood in the same place. It was a while before we moved.

It was then that we noticed what lay scattered across the dirt in the bushes, like shattered plates, broken moons. Pingüino's ripped up letter from the principal. It shone creamily in the dirt, and typewritten words jumped out despite everything (*"unbefitting... severely scaring her... third offense... We hope this finds you well..."*), and it was the awful irony of this that forced us away from the allamanda bush with its yellow flowers, from Rafi Consuelo's broken-down door, from Luis's rag-doll body that lay lifeless and bloody in the street. Because even though these things lay heavy in our hearts, there was something to be said for being relieved and guilty that we were still – amazingly – alive.

### FOUR CORPSES FOUND BURIED BY CABARET CONSTRUCTION SITE IN HAVANA

*At 7:30 A.M. this morning, four bodies were found buried beneath six inches of dirt with their eyes open. They were discovered by construction worker Thiago Hernandez when digging onsite with a spade and he struck something that felt, as he said, "hard, but not like a rock. Something that was soft on the outside, but hard on the inside." Upon unearthing the dirt further, Hernandez observed that what he had struck was an unattached human hand. He kept digging, and found four dead bodies. Three males and a female. Because their eyes were open, the specks of earth had, as he reported it, infiltrated beneath their eyelids. All of them showed signs of torture. All had their fingernails pulled. All had body parts missing, including hands, feet, fingers, and toes. There was no evidence of the fingernails nearby, although the other missing body parts were accounted for.*

*The police have identified the four victims as former University of Havana students Rafi Consuelo, Anita Valle, Pablo Padilla, and Jorge Rojas. This recent discovery of bodies is one of countless similar cases over the past few years, all of them with similar characteristics of body mutilation and dismemberment. Just last month, three bodies of known Fidel Castro sympathizers were chopped up and dumped into the sea, discovered only when the parts washed ashore.*

*At the suggestion these events could be connected, Havana chief of police Esteban Ventura has dismissed any possibility of the events relating to each other. In his official statement concerning the deaths, Ventura has said that the Havana Police Department will "investigate the matter" and that the deaths are "a horrific tragedy, one that will be examined thoroughly." The ages of the deceased are as follows: Rafi Consuelo, 21; Anita Valle, 19; Pablo Padilla, 22; Jorge Rojas, 22.*

*As for the construction site, plans for the cabaret to be built in this spot have momentarily abated, but will continue on within the next week. The discovery of the bodies has had no impact whatsoever on the morale of owner Franklin Ucker who has stated that "while the deaths are certainly unfortunate and I offer my most heartfelt condolences to the families of the victims, I have no plans of terminating construction." The cabaret will open later this fall in November.*

It wasn't front page news, just two columns on the third page of *The Havana Post.* I'm sure everyone on our street was talking about it, or grieving, though none of us would ever know. We were stuck inside for the day, pulled out of school. Luis Rodriguez's body had been cleared from the street. I'd glanced out the window in the morning and only the bloodstains remained. From afar they could have been anything. Dark oil spills from a car. Tire marks maybe.

I flipped through the whole newspaper twice and found no mention of Luis Rodriguez or the arms cache in Rafi Consuelo's house. No mention of Tío Rodrigo or his partner, Manuel. No mention of how Rafi and Anita had been missing for a month. No mention of Luis Rodriguez's body stranded in the street with three bullet wounds in his back nor of whoever had made his corpse disappear.

No one cried. No one was surprised. When Papi read the article, he shook his head and said, "That piece of work, Esteban Ventura. Everyone knows it's him who's cut up those bodies, but the newspapers can't say anything because they're censored." When Mami saw the list of the dead, and their ages right next to them, she rubbed her eyes and said, "*Los pobres Valles.* Killing themselves over whether or not she'd ever come home, and now they know, don't they? Never. Never coming back. She was only nineteen years old. I wonder if the police told them, or if they found out through the newspapers like everyone else." And Abuelo sat in his green chair as always, and muttered to himself, "It's always the people who pay. Real people. Our people this time."

The last box had been packed, and there was no need for Celia anymore. The house seemed strange without her and Mami running through the hallways with lamps or picture frames or radios in their hands, searching for a place to pack things. Instead, Mami watched a televised ballet on the couch. Papi shone his shoes in the kitchen, the brush and the towels and the polish strewn about. No one talked.

Eventually Papi went to work. He'd be breaking the news to Dulce about the big move, explaining everything to her. Celia, the mobster at the Hotel Nacional, the plantation in Oriente. He couldn't sell the shoe shop because that would attract too much attention, so he was going to hand it over to Dulce, the whole thing. "She knows how to run it anyway," he said as he went out the door. "To be honest, it's been her doing most of the work. I think she's even better than me at shining shoes. Lord knows she'll be able to keep the place organized." For a few seconds, his eyes went wistful. There would be no more warm gusts of leather wind, no more piles of mutilated shoes at work tables, no more Dulce sitting bored at her desk, flipping through magazines or licking lollipops. Things he'd called mundane. He would be paying the price for it now. I didn't know whether or not he realized it, but I didn't care because I still felt a metal bitterness in my mouth whenever I saw him or heard him speak. What I did know was those few seconds of wistfulness in his eyes. Then out the door, the screen door closing behind him.

At the table, me and Pingüino glanced at each other, waiting for the bubble to burst. Luis Rodriguez was dead and no one knew. To everyone, the stains in the street were oil spills. Tío Rodrigo wasn't a murderer. Luis Rodriguez was sleeping under his own roof. Rafi Consuelo's house remained dead and undisturbed. No one knew the truth except Tío Rodrigo, his partner Manuel, and three kids who had been hiding in the bushes, and knew only how to stay quiet. The bubble needed to burst.

It came in the form of Señora Rodriguez.

She knocked on the front door and Mami opened it.

"He's dead," Señora Rodriguez said. "Luis is dead. They killed him."

She was rushed inside and hurried onto the couch. She was given a small cup of coffee, extra sugar, and it shook in her hands as she brought it to her lips.

"Rodrigo came by this morning. He died last night. Right here on our street. In front of Rafi Consuelo's house. I heard three gunshots last night, louder than usual, but I thought they were the normal ones. I thought Luis had gone to the city to meet some friends. I never thought…"

"I'm so sorry," Mami said.

"I'm not even sure I've realized it yet," Señora Rodriguez said, her voice trembling. "It's not like he's dead, it's more that he's not alive anymore and…" She began to cry and her sobs were heartrending. "Why? – Why did they have to –? *Muerto* – Dead – *Mi pobre Luis, mi bebe*." She screamed with grief.

Abuelo gazed expressionless at her from his chair. Mami sat next to her on the couch and put her arm around her, rubbed her back like a child, waiting for her to calm down enough to speak. It was horrible. It would never end. Just screaming and screaming, and with every new scream Pingüino covered his ears, wincing. "Shhh," Mami said, "Shhh." After a while she was reduced to silent tears, dripping onto her neck, onto her hands wrinkled like an *abuela*'s. This whole time Luis had wanted to kill himself because he thought he had robbed his mother of purpose. And I realized that it was the other way around. He was dead. She was purposeless. Now she would be nothing more than burned nightgowns and wistful cigarettes by the window. Unpicked lemons growing too ripe and falling rotten to the earth. Fruit flies in the yard. The end of things.

Mami held her in her arms. "Who did it?" she said.

Señora Rodriguez shook her head. Mami offered her a tissue and she took it. "He said he wasn't even supposed to tell me anything. That the police had told him not to. They just wanted me to sit there for the rest of my life wondering where my son had gone, when he'd been killed a couple of doors down, three bullets in the back while running away. They've attributed it to 'random violence,' but I know he was lying. He knew. He knew and he wouldn't tell me. No one saw it happen. Just like with the Hotel Nacional bombings..."

Me and Pingüino avoided each other's eyes.

"But Deianeira," Señora Rodriguez continued, "it doesn't matter how it happened. Because he's dead. Not a person anymore, not my son. Just a pile of lifeless flesh somewhere, and it's not fair, because" – she began to sob again – "because he was such a beautiful boy. Even now, I can see him. Picking lemons in the backyard, using the stepladder to get to the highest ones, always talking. He wasn't always like this. Silent and moody. Secretive. He was beautiful. The most beautiful thing. And now no one will ever know."

"He doesn't have to be," Mami whispered. "He doesn't have to be dead. You can keep him beautiful. I think you can keep most things beautiful if you try."

Señora Rodriguez wiped her eyes. Then she reached into her shirt and pulled out papers. Childlike writing just like the letters Señora Valle had spread across our coffee table a few weeks ago.

"Are these the letters?" Mami said.

Señora Rodriguez nodded. "He was with Fidel. Rodrigo told me this morning. Now we know for sure."

"Mami?" I said. Pingüino was wide-eyed gazing at the letters. "Mami, did you know something?"

"No, not exactly. Señora Rodriguez and Señora Valle were finding strange letters addressed to Anita and Luis, and they wanted me to help. That's why Papi picked you up some days and took you to the shoe shop."

"I used to find them beneath the rug on the front porch every couple of days," Señora Rodriguez said. "I could never figure out what they said, because I can't read very well, but I know it was from them. The other rebels. The two boys who came to town a few weeks ago. I saw them leave it from behind the curtains, when they thought I wasn't home. He kept them in an old shoebox. I don't know what to do with them."

We stared at the letters in her hands, the yellowed paper, the letters just visible through the other side.

"Burn them." It was Abuelo who said it. He had his hands clasped in his lap. "That's what you told Señora Valle to do, wasn't it?"

"Burn them," Mami said in agreement. "Now."

The papers burned slowly. Mami went fishing through the kitchen drawers for the blue pack of matches she used for candles when the lights went out. Then we went to the backyard and huddled around the burning pile so no one would see, even though there was no one there to see it. Our next-door neighbors weren't home.

We did it on the concrete slab of our backyard, right beneath the mango trees, the redness of the mangoes shining through the leaves like non-beating hearts, watching like the rest of us. Señora Rodriguez didn't want us to read the letters, so Mami folded each piece of paper and lit the edges. There was no wind, but it took a few tries to get the matches working. Every time one of them went out, Mami threw the half-burned stick to the ground and started a new one.

The burning itself surprised me. The flames were barely there. The ashes weren't the way ashes were supposed to be. Not gray and grainy, but large and black. Peeling away like tree bark in the breeze. It crumbled so soft it could've been good enough to eat. The heat made us dizzy, drunken almost. We blinked and our eyes felt dry. In the end, all that was left was a small pile of delicate blackness, sifting windless on the concrete.

Later, after Señora Rodriguez gathered herself and went home, after Abuelo returned to his green chair, after Pingüino trudged to our room to take one last look at the bedroom closet, Mami got out the broom and the dustpan. She held the broom, I knelt on the concrete with the pan, and she swept away every last fleck of darkness from our backyard. But still I felt the flecks hiding. In the dirt of the grass and the cracks in the concrete. I beat the pan against the edge of the trashcan in the kitchen. Out the back window, everything was as still as it had been before Señora Rodriguez and her purposelessness. The hearts in the trees watched on, as dead as ever.

When night fell, there was another knock at the door. Mami and I were curled on the couch watching television. Abuelo and Pingüino were in their rooms. Papi opened the door.

"Celia?"

Mami tore her eyes from the television, but it wasn't Celia. It was Tío Rodrigo, and I went cold remembering the way he had shot Luis as he ran away. He was somber. The black-and-white police car was parked at the roadside, and Manuel was in the front seat watching our house through the window.

"Rodrigo," Papi said. He eyed Manuel in the police car. "Come in."

Tío Rodrigo stepped across the threshold and saw us on the couch. He took off his hat and rubbed his head.

"What are you doing here?" Papi asked.

"Sebastián, I'm going to have to ask you a couple questions."

"About what?"

"It would be better if we did this outside."

"What is it? Has something gone wrong?"

"Not exactly."

"What do you mean? You got your paycheck, didn't you?"

"Yes, but –"

"They didn't suspect anything, did they?"

"No, it's nothing to do with that."

"Then what is it?"

"I really think it might be better if we did this outside."

"Just spit it out."

Tío Rodrigo cleared his throat, "Very well then." He opened the door and made a motion for Manuel to come inside. Manuel lumbered out of the police car with a white box in his hands, and I recognized it. It was the white box with the red shoes. Celia's red shoes. Except the box was mangled and destroyed in Manuel's hands. Manuel handed the box to Tío Rodrigo.

"Do you know someone by the name of Celia?"

Papi gazed at the white box. "What happened?"

"She's dead, Sebastián."

Papi stared at Tío Rodrigo's face. "What do you mean? How can she be dead?"

"She's just... dead."

Papi's face contorted. He looked around the room helplessly, maybe searching for something to hold onto, but there was nothing. He sat in his own sphere of emptiness.

"Was she the prostitute?" Tío Rodrigo said, and I was surprised at the softness of his voice.

"Don't you —" Papi said, struggling. "Don't you dare. She is so much more than that."

Tío Rodrigo tried again, "Was this the girl you had an affair with?"

"Yes."

"Someone called the police yesterday night because they heard noises coming from this girl's apartment. Manuel and I — we found her body today. The room was a mess. Broken things everywhere. She was on the floor, by the window. Someone had strangled her. And next to her was this shoebox and we found a note in it. From you." Tío Rodrigo took a piece of paper from his pocket and gave it to Papi. He barely glanced at it.

"It was the mobster wasn't it? He sent someone."

"I think so. Yes."

"I've killed her," Papi said, and his voice broke. Mami walked over. She hugged him and he didn't notice.

"No, you haven't."

"But I have," Papi said, and he was bewildered with himself. His eyes were shattered just like Miguel's after the Hotel Nacional. He was crying. "I've killed her and it's my fault."

"Shhh."

"It's all my fault! It's always my fault! Why is it always my fault?"

Mami was silent, stroking his hair. Abuelo and Pingüino had emerged from their bedrooms and they were confused. I didn't bother explaining. Tío Rodrigo said something I didn't catch and then Manuel walked back to the police car with the white box.

"How am I going to live?" Papi said.

"One day at a time," Mami said. "That's how I learned."

"You didn't kill anyone."

"Neither did you."

"But it's my fault."

"It is."

"I tried, Deianeira. I tried to make things better, but I only did it for myself and I made things worse. Adela was right. All I do is destroy."

"Stop it," Mami said. "Stop it right now. Pitying yourself won't help."

"Will someone tell us what the hell is going on?" Abuelo said.

Papi walked towards the couch and Mami helped him towards it.

"Celia's dead," I said.

"Delita, I'm sorry," Papi said. "I'm so sorry. Pingüino, I'm sorry too."

Pingüino didn't seem sympathetic. "I can't even bother feeling sorry for you."

"Pingüino, be quiet," Mami said.

"How can you take his side after everything he's done?"

"Because the alternative is hating him and I'm not willing to do that. I'm not willing to love everything he's done either, but I'm willing to understand."

"I don't understand this. I don't understand any of it," Pingüino said.

"You have to try. You can't understand if you don't try."

"Sebastián," Tío Rodrigo said. "If he's killed her, then you're next."

"We'll leave in the morning," Mami promised.

"You'd better," Tío Rodrigo said. "I'm sorry, Sebastián," he said to Papi. Then he followed Manuel out the door and to his police car.

Papi wasn't listening. He stared at the note in his hands. I could read his handwriting over his shoulder.

*Para Celia. Para que me recuerdes.*
*— Sebastián Santiago*

Mami got up. "Come on, Pingüino. It's time for bed."

"I don't want to go," Pingüino said.

"I know," Mami said. "I know."

They exited, and left Papi, Abuelo, and I in the room.

Abuelo sighed. "I'm going to go pray."

"I thought you didn't pray," I said. "I thought you didn't believe in anything."

"Searching for hope is never a bad thing, especially when you don't believe in it. I would suggest you pray too, Sebastián."

Papi watched us, and the note in his hand fell to the floor. "I never said goodbye. I've just realized that. I never said goodbye."

Abuelo stood still. Then he took me by the hand, and led me to my room, and tucked me in because no one else would.

Goodbye, Señor Santiago.

*Bang! Bang! Bang!*

The three red roses bloomed. Blue and red police lights. The noise of a motor puttering to life, the police car driving away. It made a circle around the body as if it were afraid of waking it, as if it were sleeping with the three roses. In the dirt, the words shone from the pieces of paper like shattered plates, broken moons – "*We write to inform you… unbefitting… la Virgen María… severely scaring her… third offense… We hope this finds you well…*" Shallow breaths. In and out, in and out. Miguel. Pingüino. All three of us stumbling out of the allamanda bush. A leaf in Pingüino's feathery dark hair that resembled Papi's. A yellow flower crumpled and tossed away in Rafi Consuelo's uncut lawn.

We stumbled across the street. The porch light was on, yellow and bug-infested. On the top step was a half-empty, half-full jug of milk. Droplets of its whiteness glistened on the porch and the steps. It trembled in the grass like dew. I felt bad for Miguel. He'd have to walk by the body a second time to get home. He'd have to circle around the body like his father had. He'd have to try not to look at Luis Rodriguez's face smashed into the pavement, at his dead eyes, his open mouth.

Except he wouldn't. He wouldn't have to do any of those things.

We were on the porch. He was splattered onto the street. We saw it. He got up. He dusted himself off. The bullet holes were nonexistent. He stretched, scratched his own back, and when he pulled his hand away there were three red roses. Luis Rodriguez whistled *Guantanamera*. He strolled over as if it wasn't nighttime and he hadn't just been shot. All there was was the tune of it, the words echoing in my head: *Guantanamera, guajira Guantanamera / Guantanamera, guajira Guantanamera / Cultivo una rosa blanca, en junio como en enero...*

It was Christmas. In Havana, the garland must have been up, the yellow stars and the copper bells. All the streets dressed up. Even Batista would be wearing a star on his head, wrapped up in rounds and rounds of ammunition looped together.

We put our hands out.

"Here you go," Luis said. He handed each of us a rose.

We grabbed them by the stalks and the thorns pricked us, but the centers were all wrong. Each one had a sticky red bullet lodged in the center, bleeding out. They were warm. They got warmer. They were hot. They seared our fingertips.

"*¡Ay!*" we yelled.

Luis was sad. The three holes in his back bled through his front. His face was pale and dead. "I'm sorry," he said. And it wasn't just him standing there, but it was Papi too. And it was the two strangers and Fidel. And it was Celia and Tío Rodrigo and Batista and whatever the mobster must've looked like. And it was every American who had ever lived, who had ever sat like kings on their continent and thought of the little island people. And even I was there, in the background. Me with my dark blond hair and my muddy green eyes like my grandmother's.

It was all of them, everyone to be angry at and some of them apologized like Luis, but others didn't. Some stood vacant-eyed and staring like the mobster. Papi was crying and so was Celia, and I saw the finger marks on her throat as if a ghost were choking her. Fidel and Batista eyed each other before Fidel scratched his beard with his gun and Batista adjusted the Christmas star on his head. The two strangers lingered behind Fidel like bodyguards. The other Adela threaded through the crowd as if she were lost or searching for something. I stood before them carrying a burning red rose.

I wanted to throw it back at them, but I didn't. Instead, I stepped off the porch. Pingüino and Miguel disappeared. I was alone. The lawn was awash in white dew. I knelt in the dirt and dug the earth apart. I felt the mounds beneath my fingernails. I threw in the rose even though its thorns wanted to stay stuck to my fingers. The crowd watched behind me. I pushed the dirt back over top of it and somehow that was the hardest part, like the earth had gained a thousand pounds, as if each speck were the weight of a boulder.

The ground was silent. Then the rose sprouted through and it was as white as the dew. The crowd crumbled to ash. The ash blew away and it wasn't gray and grainy, but large and black. Peeling away like tree bark in the breeze. Soon the people were a delicate windless pile of black on the street. Then they were gone.

When I woke up, it was the morning of leaving and it was dark outside. The dream lent a surrealness to everything, and when I sat up it still felt like a dream. I went into the kitchen and the tile was cool against my feet, the orange of the walls was dim. Through the screen door, I saw Papi's bare back and he was shirtless and unmoving. My eyes stung because I realized what the white roses were, what José Martí had meant all those years ago when he sat in his prison cell and thought of betrayal. Sometimes people were twisted and human. Sometimes those people were presidents and sometimes they were rebels and sometimes they were family. Sometimes they meant to be horrible and sometimes they didn't. Sometimes I was one of those people too. That was the red-rose way of life. And maybe I would be upset and hate those people for a while, but it shouldn't last forever, it never should. Because I had to absorb the pain and cultivate it within myself until it was something blooming and beautiful and pure. Any old person could be uprooted and angry, but it took a sincere one to bloom even after the heart was torn out still beating. Even after everything, I would do as José Martí did once. I would grow my own white roses. In the dead of night, I planted my first seed. I sat next to Papi on the front porch. He was crying. I leaned against his shoulder, and the sun began to rise.

## 33 Goodbye

When we finally left our tiny blue house in Marianao, the sky was a deep and truthful indigo. The color of endings, the color of beginnings. I took one last look at our living room and it had been stripped of soul. The pictures gone from the mantels, the kitchen drawers half-open, all empty. The lights off. Only the big things left behind. The stove and the refrigerator sagging from years of use. The black-and-white television's screen sitting gray, the top of it already gathering dust. The couch and Abuelo's green chair sat as if they belonged in a play, like the first act was about to start, the actors were about to come onstage. There would be a mother and a father and a brother and a sister and maybe even a grandfather. And maybe they would live happily ever after. Or maybe they would all wind up dead. Either way, it was the end of imagining things. It was time to go now. We settled ourselves into Abuelo's car, which was the blue of hard candy. It was a breathless moment before Papi put the keys into the ignition. All five of us had never been in the car together before. Mami and Papi in the front seat. Pingüino, Abuelo, and I jammed into the back. It would be ten hours of this, ten hours of traveling from one side of the island to the other, ten hours for things to sink in once and for all: we were never coming back. The last thing I saw before Papi pulled away from our tiny blue house in Marianao was Abuela's white-and-green curtains through the front window. And I could have sworn that they fluttered a bit, as if somewhere within the house there was a character from the play that we had left behind, as if someone were trying to wave goodbye.

## ( *Acknowledgements* )

The first person I would like to thank is my mother. Unlike most parents, she stuck by this mess of a novel from the moment it was a collection of vignettes all the way to final edits. She even dealt with me neurotically handwriting it in the hotel bathtub when we were on vacation in Peru. Needless to say, she's been through a lot.

Second, I would like to thank everyone who has had an impact in my Literary Arts education. Thank you to Suhaila Tenly for introducing me to the art of writing. Thank you to Suzanne Supplee for teaching it to me, and for always being truthful and genuine not only in your critique, but in your approach to education as well. Thank you to the Literary Arts Class of 2016 for dealing with my extensive line edits, for being my school family, and for always being genuinely themselves. Thank you to Michael Stewart for turning everything I thought I knew about fiction on its head. Before taking your class, stories were mysterious unworkable blobs. If I now have any semblance of proficiency in storytelling, it is due to you.

Third, I would like to thank the various contributors this novel has had. My editors, Molly St. Ours and Robbie Levin, were the first to love Marianao and its world and played as much in its development as I did. I would like to thank Lucy Lopez and Suzanne Supplee for reading drafts of this book as it neared completion, as well as Catherine Rosas-Huerta and Samantha Frost for the different cover designs and for not flinching at the seventeen pages of out-of-context novel excerpts I gave them to do it. I also would like to thank Katie Mlinek for editing my book trailer, and for making it ten times more awesome than I intended it to be.

Fourth, I would like to thank the rest of my friends and family who have been supportive of my novel-related endeavors in the last two years. These include Dayana Daniyarova, Brittany Du Bois, Daniel Guarino, my father, and my brother, Javier, who giggled himself silly when he found out that Adela's brother's name was

Pingüino (which, in case you didn't know, means "Penguin" in Spanish).

Thank you also to the people who don't know this novel exists. Thank you to my grandmother, Catherine Rodriguez, who died many years ago in a sun-dappled hospital in Miami. Thank you to the Cubans who were brave in the face of Batista's regime and those who are brave now under Castro's. Thank you to José Martí for your belief in white roses. Thank you to anyone else who believes in the art of white roses too.

Adela Santiago, when she first popped in my head, was in her early twenties. She had dark blond hair and muddy green eyes, and when the Cuban Revolution came pounding into Havana, she fled to Spain where she waited for a distant lover and learned to sew her own clothing. In other words, she was my grandmother, Catherine Rodriguez, who fled Havana in 1959 and died of Alzheimer's at 60 before I had the chance to know her properly. Catherine had just finished her degree in pharmacy school when she left, and she had gotten married to one of her professors. When she finally came to the United States, she had to not only learn English, but redo all of her college education. She later became a pharmacist.

I don't remember anymore what Adela's original story was. I created her when I was fourteen and still didn't know how fiction worked. Thankfully, I thought of her again when I had to do a final project at the end of my Fiction Seminar at Brown University. It was here under the guidance of Michael Stewart that a series of vignettes bloomed about Miguel and the Hotel Nacional, Señora Rodriguez and the lemon trees, Mami in the kitchen making *ropa vieja*, *los americanos*, and Abuelo's car in Havana. Later, I reconfigured them into a novel. Originally, *The Art of White Roses* was meant to be a novel in three parts, each 150 pages long. In a panic, I finished writing the entire first part at the end of my junior year in high school and began handwriting the second part in my journal on a trip to Peru. Once I realized that the first 150 pages had a pulsating life of their own, I abandoned my 450-page journey and the result of it is what is contained in this book.

Although Adela's story is no longer my grandmother's, my grandmother played a huge part in how I visualized Cuba in the 1950s. In much the same way that I have a made-up vision of who she was as a person, I also have a made-up vision of what Cuba was. I can't pretend to know what Cuba was like and I can't pretend to know what my grandmother was like. Still, I like to

think there are bits of her scattered into this story. She is to me
what Adela's grandmother is to her: a ghost floating nearby,
smiling bittersweetly. For this reason, I dedicate this book to her.

Viviana Prado-Núñez was born in San Juan, Puerto Rico and currently lives in Reisterstown, Maryland with her mother and her dog. She has a father and half-brother who live in Puerto Rico and she visits them multiple times a year. Her writing experience includes a four-year Literary Arts program at the George Washington Carver Center for Arts and Technology, as well as attendance of a Fiction Seminar at Brown University and the Iowa Young Writers' Studio. Previously, she has been published in *Synergy*, a literary magazine, and was included in the 2014 Best Teen Writing anthology. She has won Center Stage's My America/My Baltimore Monologue contest, and has received two Gold Medals at the national level from the Scholastic Art and Writing Awards for poetry and short story. She will be attending Columbia University in the fall of 2016.

Made in the USA
Charleston, SC
16 July 2016